Question: Ho

An

Texas Grooms Wan miniseries in Harlequin Romance®.

Meet three wonderful heroines who are all looking for very special Texas men—their future husbands!

Good men may be hard to find, but these women have experts on hand. They've all signed up with the Yellow Rose Matchmakers. The oldest—and the best!—matchmaking service in San Antonio, Texas, the Yellow Rose guarantees to find any woman her perfect partner....

So, for the cutest cowboys in the whole state of Texas, read:

Only cowboys need apply...

Books in this series are:

HAND-PICKED HUSBAND by Heather MacAllister in January 1999
BACHELOR AVAILABLE! by Ruth Jean Dale in February 1999
THE NINE-DOLLAR DADDY by Day Leclaire in March 1999

Name:	Heather MacAllister (aka Heather Allison!)
Age:	Negotiable
Occupation:	Writer
Marital Status:	Currently retired from dating!
Ideal partner:	Someone I can talk with forever
Ideal date:	Anything with bagpipes and haggis

Strangest date: A friend was dating a policeman. He offered to take several of us for a ride in his patrol car. We piled in, drove around, and a call came through. He had to answer it, so he drove downtown to a really seedy area, then left us sitting in the car while he chased down the suspect. After catching him, the policeman had to call for another car, making up some story about why he already had a car full of college girls. I do not know—and do not wish to know—what he told the other policemen!

P.S. My mother does not know this!

What others have said of Heather MacAllister:

"Funny, tender, sassy. No matter what name she writes under, Heather's books are guaranteed smile-makers."
—Day Leclaire

"Heather MacAllister makes me laugh, and that's the highest accolade I can give to a fellow author. Bet she'll make you laugh, too!"
—Ruth Jean Dale

"For a good time, read Heather MacAllister!"
—Christina Dodd

Hand-Picked Husband
Heather MacAllister

TEXAS
GROOMS
WANTED!

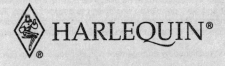

HARLEQUIN®

TORONTO • NEW YORK • LONDON
AMSTERDAM • PARIS • SYDNEY • HAMBURG
STOCKHOLM • ATHENS • TOKYO • MILAN • MADRID
PRAGUE • WARSAW • BUDAPEST • AUCKLAND

ISBN 0-373-03535-7

HAND-PICKED HUSBAND

First North American Publication 1999.

CHAPTER ONE

FACSIMILE
To: Nellie Barnett, Golden B Ranch
From: Debra Reese, Reese Ranch
Dear Nellie,
As far as I can tell, Autumn isn't planning on going back to law school this semester. It wouldn't hurt for you to give that boy of yours a nudge in her direction. You can't expect her to wait forever.
We're leaving for the Menger this afternoon.
Happy New Year!

FAX
To: Debra Reese, Reese Ranch
From: Nellie Barnett, Golden B Ranch
Dear Debra,
I have nudged. Clay is spending the night at the Menger with friends. Good luck, and happy New Year!

AUTUMN Reese stifled a yawn and signaled the waiter for another cup of coffee. Why did the San Antonio Rodeo Swine Auction Program Committee always schedule their kickoff for New Year's Day? At least she'd managed to convince them to change it to a brunch from the breakfast it had been in years past.

5

Autumn's mother poked her in the ribs. "Perk up and smile, honey. There's Clayton."

"I'm not perking for anything but coffee." She stared at the bottom of her cup. "And I sincerely hope there's a pot perking for me."

"People are watching," Debra Reese said without moving her lips and still smiling herself. "You can't continue to pretend that you haven't seen Clay without there being *talk*."

"There's always talk."

"And don't you forget it."

As her mother raised her hand to wave at Clayton Barnett, their ranching neighbor to the west, Autumn sent a dutiful smile of acknowledgment his way, saving her real smile for the waiter, who was now weaving his way around the tables in the Menger Hotel banquet room with a pot of coffee.

"Clay!" her mother called in a voice guaranteed to draw the attention of anyone who hadn't noticed Clay's tardy arrival. "We saved you a place."

Autumn cringed. "What if he doesn't want to sit here, Mom?"

Debra turned to her daughter in surprise. "Where else would he want to sit?"

And that pretty much summed up the attitude of their ranching community, Autumn thought. Somehow it had been determined that she and Clay were meant for each other, and that was that.

Autumn watched Clay succumb to the inevitable and begin making his way toward them. They'd grown up as next-door neighbors, or as close as next door got in rural Texas. It wasn't as though she had anything against him. He'd become a good-looking man and was by all accounts a decent human being. She'd known him forever. She'd worked with him, fought with him, competed with him and had even gone to the same college with him.

But did that mean she was supposed to spend the rest of her life with him?

The waiter and Clay arrived about the same time. "Morning, Miz Reese. Autumn."

"Clay!" her mother fluttered. "I haven't seen you since Christmas."

"And the week just flew by." Autumn nudged her cup toward the waiter. Autumn's mother nudged her.

"Go ahead and leave the pot," Clay instructed the man, and folded his long legs under the table.

The waiter did so—before pouring Autumn's coffee. With an irritated look at Clay, she lifted the heavy thermal pot and splashed coffee into her cup.

Grinning, Clay shoved his cup and saucer across the table. Because Autumn was under the watchful eye of her mother, she poured coffee for Clay, as well, instead of telling him to pour his own, which she would have done had they been alone.

The coffee was good and strong, and hot, Autumn knew from her prior cup. She added cream, partly for the taste and partly to cool off the liquid. She drank a good gulp, hoping Clayton would follow suit and burn his tongue since he took his coffee black.

He did.

"Mmm." He winced and replaced the cup in the saucer.

Autumn smiled serenely, also noting his bloodshot eyes.

Apparently, her mother did, as well. "Did you have a party to go to last night, Clay?" she asked after a quick chastising look at a silent Autumn.

"Yes, ma'am, and I'm not real pleased with the person responsible for moving the meeting to brunch, which is some made-up meal, instead of an honest breakfast. Breakfast would have capped off the evening just right." He downed a goblet of orange juice.

Autumn pointedly looked around the crowded room. "We have a lot better attendance because the meeting was moved to eleven o'clock," she said without admitting that she was the one who'd been responsible for the moving. "It's just plain silly to ignore the fact that New Year's Eve is the night before. This way, people can actually get some sleep before the meeting, and it'll be over in time for the football games."

"As for sleep, I suppose it depends on how great your party was." He grinned.

Autumn drank her coffee. She hadn't had a date for New Year's Eve. Any single men of her acquaintance no doubt assumed she would be with Clay. "Mom and I heard your party last night."

"But we were awake anyway," Debra inserted quickly.

Heaven forbid Clay might think Autumn was criticizing him. She poured herself more coffee.

Since she was on the brunch committee and in charge of decorations, she and her mother had spent the night at the Menger. Most of that night had been spent filling the pink, white and black helium balloons that were tied to the ceramic pig centerpieces.

Happy New Year.

"Sorry if we were a little rowdy. Seth and Pete and Luke and I don't get to see much of each other except at rodeo time. We had a lot of catching up to do."

"So tell us all the news," Debra invited.

"Well…Seth and Claire have a brand-new baby boy, and so do Luke and Livie."

"Baaabies." Autumn's mother sighed and gave Autumn a gooey look.

Autumn tensed. Not baby talk. Not in front of Clay.

"There's just something about holding a baby in your arms.… I remember when you two were babies. Clayton, you were such an active little boy. Always crawling, always moving. Autumn, you were a little dumpling."

"Gee, thanks, Mom." Autumn set her coffee cup down.

"Well, you're certainly not a dumpling now, is she, Clay?"

Their eyes met, and bloodshot though his were, they managed to take a quick inventory.

Fortunately, the servers set a platter of eggs, sausage, bacon, ham, hash brown potatoes, grits and biscuits with cream gravy in front of them before Clay took the opportunity to make a snide remark.

Autumn inhaled. The one meal of the year where she inverted the U.S. government's food pyramid. She immediately went for the biscuits and gravy.

"She'll be a dumpling if she eats all this," Clay said.

Autumn stopped, the fork halfway to her mouth. Gravy plopped onto her plate.

"Why, the portions are enormous. Of course Autumn won't eat all this." Debra virtuously nibbled on a piece of dry toast from the bread basket.

Autumn ate the bite of biscuit and gravy anyway, but it didn't taste nearly as good.

Debra had been a rancher's daughter and wife long enough to know that a woman shouldn't get between a man and his food and she directed most of her small talk toward Autumn. However, that small talk was carefully edited to elicit answers designed to impress Clayton.

"Autumn, you and the committee did a wonderful job planning the brunch today," Debra said.

Clay raised an eyebrow, obviously figuring out the culprit responsible for the time change.

"Thanks, Mom."

"She's worked so hard, Clay."

"The food's great," he said.

Autumn hadn't had anything to do with the food. The brunch was catered by the hotel's kitchen and the menu was the same as it had been for years. Clayton knew this, of course. She smiled thinly.

"And the decorations are just precious," Debra continued, oblivious to the looks Autumn and Clay exchanged. "The kickoff meeting is so important because it sets the tone for the whole swine auction. It was an honor to be asked to be on this committee. Usually, you have to work in the trenches for at least five years before they let you move up to one of the important committees. I'm so proud of her. Maybe next year she can move on to one of the cattle auction committees.''

"She deserves it," Clay said. "Nobody can fill balloons like Autumn."

"Mom helped," Autumn said in warning. She didn't want her mother caught in the cross fire between them.

"Did you bake the cookies, too, Miz Reese?'' Clay picked up one of the pig-shaped sugar cookies that were the brunch favors.

"Oh, my, no. Autumn—''

''*Autumn* baked them?'' he interrupted.

Autumn's silverware clanked against the china plate. "No. I found a bakery to design a custom cookie for us.''

Clay relaxed. "Well, that's a…''

"Relief" was the word he'd been about to say. Autumn narrowed her eyes.

''…a great idea,'' he substituted. But if her mother hadn't been here, he wouldn't have.

Autumn's cooking failures were legendary. In self-defense, she'd gone out for barrel racing instead of competing in the culinary arts portion of the rodeo. She was as good a barrel racer as she was as bad a cook.

Mercifully, the business meeting started shortly after that. Autumn gave Clay a frigid smile and turned her chair toward the podium.

''I'm mighty glad to see y'all out here this mornin' for our program-sales kickoff,'' began a man wearing a belt with the grand champion buyer's huge buckle. "My name's Fred Chapman and I'm the head of today's doings." There was good-natured laughter and applause. "Before we get down to assigning the sales groups, I want to lay a few stats on you. You know, we have both a lot of fun and a goodly little competition raising money." There was more laughter.

Autumn and Clay glanced at each other. These people thought they'd seen competition? They hadn't seen anything yet.

"But when it comes down to it, we're doing this for the kids. Last year, we raised..."

Since Autumn already knew how much scholarship money had been raised, her mind wandered during Fred's pep talk. For the next month, she and her group, Hogs and Kisses, would scour San Antonio persuading businesses to contribute to the Livestock Show and Rodeo education fund.

Clay would be doing the same, and Autumn was determined that Hogs and Kisses would raise more money than his group, High on the Hog.

The meeting didn't take long because the men wanted to get home in time to watch the New Year's Day football games on TV. When Fred's speech was over, the crowd lined up to register their groups, and Autumn's mother drifted away to talk with friends.

"You might as well give up now, Autumn," a familiar voice murmured in her ear.

Clay was behind her in the line. "You wish, Clay, 'cause that's the only way you'll win."

He laughed, but it was a tired laugh without the usual sharpness.

Autumn turned to face him. "Do you feel as bad as you look?"

Clay grimaced and ran a hand over his jaw. He'd missed a few spots shaving. "Probably."

"Then maybe I'd better call an ambulance."

"Not unless I've eaten some of your cooking."

She eyed him. "You *are* tired if you're falling back on cooking insults."

"Haven't seen you much lately. Guess I'm out of practice." He smiled crookedly and drew his hands up to his waist. "How are you and your mom getting along?"

Autumn automatically scanned the room until she found her mother and her group of friends. Debra was smiling as she talked. "She's a lot better. This was the second Christmas since Dad died and it was definitely easier than last year."

"I miss your dad," Clay said. "A lot of people do."

"Yeah." Autumn turned until she faced the sign-up tables again. She still got misty-eyed when thinking about her father and didn't want Clay to see.

"So...are you planning to go back to law school any time soon?"

Good question. The longer she was out of school, the less enthusiastic she felt about going back. "Maybe this summer," she answered just as they reached Jackie Dutton at the table.

"Hey, Autumn...Clay. Let me find your packet."

Before Autumn could stop her, Jackie went to the B section and pulled out Clay's packet.

"Oh, would you look at this?" Shaking her head, she uncapped a pen. "They left Autumn's name off the list. I am *sorry*. I can't imagine how that happened."

"Because I'm not with Clay's group," Autumn told her when it was obvious Clay wasn't going to.

"You're not with High on the Hog?" Jackie looked incredulous.

"She's going to wish she was." Clay took his packet and winked at Autumn.

"I'm with Hogs and Kisses," Autumn said.

"But…" Jackie looked from one to the other. "You two aren't on the same committee?"

The streaked-blond woman next to Jackie leaned over. "What's the problem?"

"Clay and Autumn are on different committees."

"Computers." The blonde rolled her eyes. "You just can't trust them."

"It's okay." Autumn forced herself to smile. "We didn't sign up to be on the same committee."

Both women's eyes widened. "Why not?" they asked in unison.

Autumn gritted her teeth. *Because we're not a couple, we've never been a couple, and we're never going to be a couple. Can't you people get it through your heads?*

"Because this year, it's the girls against the guys," Clay said with an easy smile. "The High on the Hog men against the Hogs and Kisses ladies.

Now, if this is everything I need, then I guess I'll see y'all later.'' He nodded his head and strode off.

Autumn resented the fact that he'd come up with an answer that did nothing to squash the persistent belief that he and Autumn were eventually going to get married.

Jackie sighed after Clay. ''There goes one good-looking man.''

''His eyes are bloodshot.''

''But there's nothing wrong with his backside. And that is one fine—'' Jackie broke off and blinked. ''You are so lucky, Autumn.''

Autumn drew a deep breath. ''Clay and I aren't dating.''

''Well, of course not.'' Jackie handed Autumn her packet. ''Why would you two need to date?''

Autumn gave up, took her packet and went to find her mother.

Mistake. It was obvious that her mother and friends had been watching Clay and Autumn as they stood in line. Autumn greeted them and steeled herself for the inevitable.

''Autumn, your mom told us that you and Clay haven't set a date yet.'' A silver-haired woman with turquoise earrings smiled expectantly.

People had stopped being subtle. ''We aren't going to set a date.''

Several pairs of eyes widened. ''You're not eloping!''

''Clay and I aren't engaged.''

''Well, not officially,'' Debra said, patting Autumn's arm.

Not even for her mother would Autumn maintain the fiction. "Not in any way."

"So you're going to wait until after you finish your schooling. Very wise," the silver-haired woman said.

There was a general nodding of heads, then everyone got sappy smiles on their faces and Autumn knew Clay was in the vicinity.

Go away, she thought.

Wonder of wonders, he passed by without speaking to her. But then she had to endure the curious looks. Holding up her packet, she explained, "We've got a bet going on who can raise the most money. Now, how much can I put you down for, Mr. Perry?"

FACSIMILE
To: Nellie Barnett, Golden B Ranch
From: Debra Reese, Reese Ranch
Nellie, dear, were you aware that Autumn and Clay are not on the same committee? From what she said, I don't think he asked her. She hasn't mentioned the Buyers' Ball. Even though I know Clay will take her, it would be nice if he observed the proprieties and asked her. We don't want any misunderstandings.

Deb

FAX
To: Debra Reese, R. Ranch
From: Nellie Barnett, Golden B
Debra, dearest, Clay couldn't very well ask Autumn to be on his committee

when she'd already formed her own. And
by the way, she could have asked him to
be on hers.

Nel

During the next two weeks, Autumn and her committee contacted the businesses of San Antonio. So
did Clay. He got larger donations but not as many.
Autumn's strategy was to go for more modest
amounts from smaller companies, like local beauty
parlors and dress shops, but that meant she had to
sign up more of them.

"Mom, I think we've asked every business in San
Antonio," Autumn groaned. "And Clay's group is
still ahead." She leafed through the newspaper at
breakfast on the Saturday they were due to meet for
a progress report. Maybe there was someplace they'd
missed.

Debra looked up from the section of paper she was
reading. "Autumn, have you considered…maybe not
trying so hard to beat Clay?"

Autumn nearly gagged on her coffee. "Are you
saying I should let him win?"

"No! Not *let* him win." Debra looked away. "Just
don't beat him."

Which was the same thing. "Forget it."

"A man has his pride."

"And what have I got?"

Debra raised an eyebrow. "Not a man, at this
point."

Autumn raised the paper. "So?"

There was a sigh. "Autumn, you don't encourage

him at all. Anybody but Clay would think you weren't interested in him. Even though you have an understanding, you shouldn't take him for granted.''

It would do no good to tell her mother that she wasn't interested in Clay. "He hasn't encouraged *me*. I think *he's* not interested."

"Don't be silly." Debra also retreated behind her newspaper. "He waited all this time for you."

"Yes, I heard about those women he brought home while he was waiting."

"Well, dear, he is a very attractive man. You can't expect—"

"Mom?" Autumn broke in, changing the subject. "Have you ever heard of the Yellow Rose Matchmakers? It's a dating agency.'' She'd spotted a discreet advertisement with a rose-vine border next to the wedding announcements. She must have missed it before because she usually avoided reading them.

"A dating agency? No…wait. I'll bet that's Willie Eden's business. She and her grandson own it. Why?"

Autumn folded the newspaper, gulped down the last of her coffee and grabbed her purse. "Because I haven't asked them for a contribution yet.'' She glanced at her watch. "If I hurry, I can stop by and still make the meeting on time."

URGENT FACSIMILE
To: N. Barnett
From: D. Reese
Nellie! Autumn thinks Clay isn't interested in her! I

tried to convince her otherwise, but I've got to tell you, Clay inviting that woman down at Thanksgiving didn't make it easy.

Debra, I keep telling you that Kristin is just an old school friend who now knows life as a ranch wife wouldn't suit her. Stop worrying.

N.

CHAPTER TWO

FACSIMILE
To: N. Barnett, Golden B
From: D. Reese, Reese Ranch
How can I stop worrying? They haven't seen each other for two weeks. Autumn is on her way over to Yellow Rose—remember that nice lady we met and her grandson?

Debra

FAX
To: D. Reese, Reese Ranch
From: N. Barnett, Golden B
I've put a bug in Clay's ear.

Nellie

IT WAS a lovely mid-January day, cool enough so she could wear her new red suede jacket, and dry with a clear blue sky. Autumn drove through town, avoiding the tourists lining up to tour the Alamo, and entered an older residential area of San Antonio.

Yellow Rose Matchmakers was located at 10 Bluebonnet Drive, in a charming Victorian house painted yellow with white trim. A white picket fence surrounded the yard, making an old-fashioned statement among the unfenced neighboring yards.

Autumn parked her black Ford Bronco on the

street next to a mailbox hand-painted with yellow roses, then went to push open the gate. Something about the act of stepping through the gate and latching it behind her made Autumn feel as though she had stepped into another time.

She'd climbed the porch steps and rung the doorbell before she stopped to consider that it was still fairly early on a Saturday morning and the agency might not be open yet, or even at all. She was just about to turn away when a shadow appeared behind the frosted-glass door and it swung open.

"It's about time, Hector. Just because you're my cousin's son doesn't mean—you're not Hector."

"No. Sorry."

The woman, short and full-figured, wearing her salt-and-pepper hair in a bun, reminded Autumn of the wife of Clay's ranch foreman. The no-nonsense tone in her voice had prompted the automatic apology.

"Well, who are you?"

"I'm Autumn Reese, from the Junior Swine Auction Education Committee." Autumn held up a copy of the magazine-size program from last year's auction. "I was wondering if Yellow Rose Matchmakers might be interested in contributing to the committee this year." Autumn flipped through the program so the woman could see the ads contributors were entitled to.

"Pigs, eh?"

Autumn nodded. "Cows are by invitation only, chickens aren't compelling, and I'm allergic to sheep."

"I'm not so sure Miss Willie would want to be associated with pigs."

Prepared for this reaction, Autumn whipped out a batch of adorable photos of cute baby pigs. Donated by a professional photographer, they featured pigs with wings, pigs dressed in kilts, pigs among flowers—anything to negate the image of pigs wallowing in a trough.

As had so many others, the woman cooed.

"Money donated goes to the education fund so all exhibitors receive a minimum amount for their pig at auction. The kids use the profits from selling their animals to fund their education."

"Weeell...let's talk. You don't see Hector out there, do you?"

Autumn dutifully looked around. Her Bronco was the only vehicle in sight. She shook her head.

The woman muttered something in Spanish. "You try to give them a break and they let you down." Opening the door wider, she gestured for Autumn to follow her inside.

Walking through the door, she experienced the same stepping-back-in-time feeling she'd had when she'd come through the gate, only more intense. A huge bouquet of yellow roses in a vase on the foyer table caught her eye immediately. Autumn stopped to smell them before following the woman into a parlorlike reception area.

Except for the brass plaque announcing Yellow Rose Matchmakers by the front door, there was nothing that resembled an office about the house. The only way Autumn knew she was in the right place was because framed photographs of smiling couples—presumably satisfied clients—covered the walls.

"I'm Maria Perez," the woman said when they settled themselves on a blue velvet sofa. "Now, I don't own this business and can't speak for Miss Willie, but she depends on me for advice. How much money are we talking?"

"The committee will be grateful for whatever amount you care to donate. However, there are certain donor levels if you wish to be acknowledged in the program."

Since Autumn had given this speech several times a day for the past two weeks, she took the opportunity to study the photographs as she talked and Maria looked through the program magazine. Never in her life had Autumn considered signing up with a dating agency. But there must have been two dozen wedding pictures on the walls.

"Miss Willie's never had a failure."

"I beg your pardon?"

Maria had caught her staring. She gestured to the photographs. "These are people Miss Willie and Wanda—she helps Miss Willie out—these are people they've brought together. They have a gift."

"They do?"

Maria nodded her head. "Course that was in the days before the computer, when Miss Willie handpicked her clients. She was so good, people convinced her to become a professional matchmaker. So many people came to her, it was either turn them away or get help. That's when Wanda came here.

But then Miss Willie's grandson convinced her to get some computers. That's not the kind of help they need, if you ask me. Ain't nothing been the same since we got those machines. But you know people. Always in a hurry.''

"Yes," Autumn said slowly. "How...how does your business work?"

Maria set aside Autumn's program and opened the huge scrapbook that lay on the coffee table. The first pages were laminated forms. "You fill these out so the computer knows what kind of person you are. Then we type all this stuff into a program Miss Willie's grandson paid way too much for and the computer picks your perfect match—or at least the three men you're most likely to get along with."

"And how does the computer do?" Autumn was only making conversation, of course.

Maria shrugged and waved her hand back and forth. "Computers only know what you tell them. For example, if you tell them you don't want nobody too short, then they won't give you a short person even though he may be as wonderful as my Aldo, may he rest in peace.''

"Then what happens?"

Maria laughed. "What happens next is up to you."

Autumn stared down at the application and was seriously tempted. How wonderful to date someone who didn't think she was destined to become the next Mrs. Clayton Barnett. How wonderful to date anyone at all. Living at the ranch made it difficult to meet eligible men even without the handicap of her mother constantly all but announcing her engagement.

Besides, if she attended the Past Champion Buyers' Ball with someone other than Clay, *that* would give people something to talk about.

She fingered the pages. "Do…do you screen your applicants?"

Maria looked horrified. "What kind of a place do you think this is? We don't take just anybody." She pointed to the form. "You got to tell us where you live, where you work, and let me tell you, we're gonna run a credit check." She smiled. "You interested? We get a lot of new people this time of year because of the rodeo. Ranchers come to town and sign up."

"I'm not sure I'd want to date a rancher."

"Then you put that on the form."

Autumn inhaled, seriously tempted. Before she came to a decision, the doorbell chimed.

"That must be Hector." Maria levered herself off the sofa cushion. "Look at that." She jabbed a finger at her watch. "Twenty-five minutes late. It's a good thing Miss Willie isn't here." Maria marched toward the door, still talking. "Hector, you better knock another ten percent off, and those upstairs windows had better—you're not Hector!"

"No, ma'am."

Autumn's head snapped up and she hurriedly closed the book.

"I'm Clayton Barnett and I'm here to invite you to contribute to the—"

"Pigs again? I got a pig lady in there already." Maria hooked her thumb over her shoulder.

Hat in hand, Clay peered around the door.

As if he hadn't recognized her Bronco parked out front, Autumn fumed as she forced a smile. "Hi, Clay."

"Autumn. Fancy meeting you here."

So original. "I got here first."

"But how was I to know you were asking for a donation?" He smiled first at her, then at Maria who was clearly affected by the tall rancher and his patented aw-shucks grin. "I thought you might have been here as a client." He walked into the parlor, his appearance making it look frilly and feminine.

The wedding portraits stopped him cold. Autumn thought they might.

"Actually, I *am* considering it," she said, just to see his reaction.

There was the pop of an engine backfiring.

"Hector!" Maria stomped out onto the porch and shouted, "It's about time you got here. Drive that truck around back." Her voice faded as she went out to scold the tardy Hector.

Clay made a tsking sound. "Buying a donation?"

"Not at all." Autumn opened the scrapbook again and flipped through the pages explaining about Yellow Rose Matchmakers. She blinked at the rate sheet, but then again, the agency promised to keep searching and matching until their clients were satisfied. "I'm going to sign up."

"You're kidding." Clay sat on the sofa next to her.

Autumn scooted over. "Why? They screen the applicants, you fill out a detailed profile, and the computer fixes you up. Very efficient."

He studied the profile forms. "I don't know... these forms ask a lot of questions. You might not want some guy you date to know the answers. That's always assuming that the computer can possibly match you to anyone."

"Of course it'll find a match!"

He leaned back and grinned. "I don't know, Autumn. Your bio is likely to freeze that computer right up."

She glared at him. "Anyone matched with you would demand a refund!"

"Anyone matched with me would give the Yellow Rose ladies a bonus."

He was insufferable.

"Prove it," she challenged him. "Sign up."

Laughing, he shook his head. "I don't need to prove anything."

But Autumn did. If she showed up at the ball with another man, that would be good, but if *both* she and Clay came with others, it would be great. "Dare ya."

It was a taunt from their childhood.

Clay raised an eyebrow.

"I dare you to bring your match to the Champion Buyers' Ball." Autumn was counting on his competitive streak where she was concerned.

For a moment, she didn't think he'd agree, then he slowly nodded. "Okay. But only if you'll do the same."

Autumn stuck out her hand and grinned. "Deal."

They were shaking on their deal when Maria returned.

She was more than happy to sign them up. "Fill out these forms, front and back." She sat Autumn and Clay at a table in one of the offices. "You going to want a video?"

"You didn't mention a video," Autumn pointed out.

Maria waved her hands. "Don't get me started on videos. I don't like 'em. People don't look good in videos. The camera makes them nervous. Besides, the machine isn't working. My cousin, Ramon, is fixing it."

"We don't need a video," Clay assured her.

"Good." Maria smiled at them. "Holler if you have questions. I'm going to check on Hector and make sure he cleans all the way into the corners on those windows. And as long as he's up there, he should clear out the gutters."

"Hector is going to wish he hadn't taken this job," Clay said as Maria hurried off.

"Hector should have been on time. Speaking of which, we're going to have to hurry if we don't want to be late to the meeting." Actually, they probably would be late, but Fred Chapman was notoriously lax about starting on time.

"This doesn't look like it'll take much time to fill out." Clay was already halfway down the first page.

Autumn was stuck on the weight question. Should she put her actual weight or the weight she planned to be before the first match? "Wait until you get to the hard questions." Weight wouldn't be a hard question for Clay. He was a nice triangular shape. So was Autumn, only the triangle was more inverted than she liked.

"What hard questions?"

She looked at him. "Politics? Religion?"

"I just put yes."

Autumn rolled her eyes. "You're supposed to tell what your politics are and which religion."

"Okay, ndb and Texas."

"What is 'ndb'?"

"None of your...business."

"Clay! Just put conservative."

"I'm not all that conservative."

"Okay, try this." Autumn thought a moment. "You're at a Dallas Cowboys game and the 'Star-Spangled Banner' is being played by the Texas A&M University Marching Band. The man next to you refuses to stand, citing freedom of speech. What do you do?"

"I'll freedom-of-speech him to his feet!"

Autumn pointed to the blank on the form. "Conservative. And Texas isn't a religion."

He looked at her in mock outrage. "Don't you go saying that around just anybody."

"Be serious."

"I am."

"Remember that the computer only knows what you tell it," she said, quoting Maria.

"So what are you putting down?" He turned her paper before she could stop him. "Hey—under Sports you put no."

"I don't like sports."

"Yes, you do. You ride, you rope, and you were a pretty fair barrel racer."

"My barrel-racing days are past and the rest is work, not sport. Besides, I don't want some man who'll plop down in front of a big-screen television, click to a football game and call it a date just because he sprang for imported beer."

Clay eyed her. "Have you had dates like that?"

She turned her paper back around. "Never more than once."

"So, what kind of dates do you like?"

The overly casual tone caught her attention. She blinked.

When she didn't answer right away, Clay tapped the paper. "It's number fourteen on the list."

"Oh." Maybe he just wanted dating pointers. "I like dates with an activity and then going someplace for coffee or a meal afterward. I don't like dinner, then a movie. I like the movie first."

"So...you still try to eat the jumbo tub of popcorn so you can get a refill and make yourself sick?"

Autumn smiled with remembered embarrassment and flipped her hair over her shoulder. "I'm not sixteen anymore."

"No." Clay's answering smile faded. He cleared his throat and stared down at his paper. Autumn did the same. They worked in silence until Clay let out a low whistle. "I see potential problems here."

"Where?"

"Page three, the part about describing yourself. That's where people will cheat."

"Why? Why go to all this trouble and cheat?"

"Maybe 'cheat' is the wrong word. What I mean is, they're going to put down the character traits they'd *like* to have, rather than the ones they actually do have."

"But *we* wouldn't do that."

"No way." Clay shook his head. "We'll be completely honest."

They looked at each other.

"When we finish, you can read mine and I'll read yours," Autumn said.

"Deal."

Finishing took longer than they thought. Autumn was very conscious that Clay would be reading her descriptions of such topics as her favorite way to spend an evening, her idea of a perfect day, her pet peeves and her goals and ambitions.

He completed his form before she did, probably because he wasn't trying to think of alternate answers for pet peeves. Autumn's current pet peeve was Clay.

Now as for goals and ambitions... Autumn realized her life's goal had been to convince people that it wasn't carved in stone that she would settle down, marry Clay and merge the ranches.

She'd gone to law school because, yes, the law, as it pertained to ranching, had interested her when she'd studied ranch management, but even more because the length of study required would take her away from San Antonio for several years.

She glanced at Clay, wondering how he stood it. Since he had no brothers or sisters, he'd known his whole life that he would live on the Golden B and run it after his parents retired. The only choice available to him had been whom he'd run it with, and even that had been taken away from him.

Autumn stared at the personality profile, but she was remembering her seventeenth birthday. Clay and his parents had come for dinner. Autumn's present had been her first car, a used one, and they had gone to the garage after dinner so Clay could check out the engine.

It was one of those clear, cold nights when every sound carried for miles. Both their fathers had stepped out onto the porch to smoke their cigars. They'd been talking and Autumn hadn't paid attention until she heard her name and Clay's.

The men had been discussing repairs to the fencing between their properties on the east pasture.

"You know, we could just leave it," Hank Barnett had said. "We're going to be mingling stock eventually. Might as well start now and use the money elsewhere."

Ben, Autumn's father, gave a loud crack of laughter. "We'll be mingling stock in more ways than one!"

Hank joined him, then added, "I hope those two kids don't get their hormones all to jumpin' and quit school before they finish."

"Autumn's got a good head on her shoulders. She'll keep Clay in line."

"Clay's almost eighteen. It's not her head he's concerned with!"

Autumn had been horrified. Clay was staring under the hood of her car with an unnatural intensity and she knew he'd heard, as well. Neither one of them said anything, so they both heard her father's next words.

"Clay's a fine boy. I'll be proud to claim him as a son-in-law."

Autumn's heart had pounded so hard that she missed the exact words said next, but the gist was clear: the two families assumed that she and Clay would eventually marry and were planning on a merger of the two ranches. From the tone of the conversation, it was clear that this was a long-held assumption.

She and Clay had stared at each other before Clay had carefully closed the car hood. Nothing had been the same between them after that.

Autumn could hardly blame him. He was the only son, bound by tradition and economics. He ought to be able to choose his wife instead of having one forced on him. She didn't want to be forced on anybody. She wanted Clay to have a choice, and she wanted one, too.

But he was a Texas gentleman through and through. There was no way he'd marry first and make it look like he'd jilted her. No, it was up to Autumn to find someone and free Clay from his obligation. The problem was that she hadn't found anybody she could contemplate marrying yet.

"Aren't you finished with that thing yet?" Clay complained. "I'm telling you, none of this matters if a person doesn't like the way you look. Within thirty seconds, you'll know if it's a go, or a no go."

Autumn gave him a disgusted look. "We don't all judge people by your shallow standards."

"It's a fact of life." He plucked her paper from between her fingers. "You don't need to worry about it, by the way."

"Why not?"

Clay looked up from reading her profile. In a heartbeat, his expression changed from looking at her as a childhood friend to the way a grown man looks at a woman he desires.

As her eyes widened, Clay's lids lowered slightly and his gaze scorched over her. To her acute embarrassment, Autumn felt her cheeks heat.

A corner of Clay's mouth twitched and he went back to reading her profile.

There'd been a compliment in there somewhere, but she wasn't comfortable with that sort of compliment from Clay. She was comfortable with verbal jabs and sarcastic remarks from Clay. She was comfortable competing with Clay. She was comfortable ignoring him. How did he expect her to ignore a look like that?

"What is this 'sentimental, serious and tolerant' garbage?" Clay scoffed.

That was more like it. "I *am* sentimental, serious and tolerant."

"Where's stubborn?"

"I am *not* stubborn. I'm focused."

Clay snorted. "And 'sensitive'? You don't have a sensitive bone in your body." He erased and changed some of the personality traits she'd checked off.

"You turn this in and you'll be matched with a dadgum poet."

Autumn narrowed her eyes and grabbed for Clay's profile. Just what wondrous traits had he given himself?

"'*Affectionate*'? Explain to me how a man who gave me a timing belt one Christmas can be described as affectionate?"

He looked puzzled—and a little hurt. "But you needed a new timing belt, and you'd spent all your money on Christmas presents. I didn't want you to get stranded on the road somewhere between here and Fort Worth."

He'd done the replacement himself, she remembered. And it had been a relief not to have to worry on the drive back to school. "That's being considerate," she allowed. "I'm changing affectionate to considerate. Now, where's arrogant?"

"Hey!"

But Autumn's attention had been caught by something else. For his dreams and goals, Clay had simply written that he wanted to make sure he maintained the family's ranch so he could leave it to his children.

And really, what other goal could he have? Yet if Autumn didn't get out of the way so Clay could find a wife, then he'd never *have* children.

She skimmed over the rest, made a few alterations, her eyebrows rising when he described his ideal mate. "You're looking for a woman who's not afraid to 'work hard, play hard and love hard'?"

He shrugged. "I thought it was kind of catchy. A lot better than a 'life partner'."

That was what she'd written. "I was trying to find a way to say that I don't want a man who's going to boss me around."

"I think we've got that covered by mentioning that you're strong-willed and independent."

"You can't put that. I'll either get a wimp or a Neanderthal."

"Well, no, actually, I said you wanted a man who wasn't afraid to be a man and to let you be a woman."

"Give me that!" Autumn stretched across the table and tried to grab the paper from him.

Laughing, Clay easily held it out of her reach.

That was how Maria found them. "You two finished?"

"Yes," Clay said.

"No," Autumn said, and retrieved her profile.

She erased Clay's macho comment and rewrote "life partner".

"You'll be sorry," he murmured as they handed Maria their forms.

"Okay," Maria said. "I got to type all this information into the computer. You can pick up your matches on Monday."

"*Monday*?" Autumn didn't want to wait until Monday.

"There's just me in the office today and I'm off at noon. I'll type as fast as I can."

"Did you check off 'impatient' on the personality profile?" Clay asked.

Autumn glared at him.

"Thank you, ma'am." Clay stood. "Monday will

be fine. We've still got that meeting to go to, Autumn.''

Right. Autumn checked her watch. They were going to be at least twenty minutes late. Even worse, they would arrive at the same time. She sighed, then brightened when she visualized everyone's faces when she showed up at the Buyers' Ball with someone other than Clay.

CHAPTER THREE

FAX
To: Debra Reese, Reese Ranch
From: Nellie Barnett, Golden B Ranch
Dear Debra,
Clay is in a very good mood. How's Autumn?
Fingers crossed, *Nellie*

FACSIMILE
To: Nellie Barnett, Golden B
From: Debra Reese, Reese Ranch
Dear Nellie,
Everything's sunny here. She acts like
she's got a secret. Do you suppose this
is IT?

Holding my breath,
D.

AUTUMN weighed arriving when the Yellow Rose opened on Monday morning and appearing overeager with the desire to nail down a contribution from them before Clay could. Beating out Clay won.

Promptly at nine o'clock, Autumn turned down Bluebonnet Drive and parked her Bronco. In her rearview mirror, she saw a red pickup truck pull close to the curb behind her. Clay. It figured.

He was talking on his cell phone, so instead of waiting for him, Autumn pushed open the gate and ran up the porch steps.

The outer doors of the Yellow Rose were propped open with a ceramic cat doorstop. Through the glass inner door, Autumn could see Maria in the reception area, but she was turned away.

As Autumn opened the door, she heard Maria calling out to someone in the back. "I'm telling you, Miss Willie, call my sister's middle girl, Amalia. She's the best wallpaper hanger in San Antonio. I sewed the flower girls' dresses for her wedding, so she'll give you a discount."

The receptionist smiled up at her, but before she could ask if she could help, Maria turned back around, saw Autumn and looked at the grandfather clock across the hall. "Boy, you sure are eager."

"Actually, I wondered if you'd had a chance to ask the owner if she's willing to contribute to the education fund or do you need me to speak to her?"

"No need. I already did and she's gonna go the whole hog." Maria looked at the receptionist and they both laughed.

Autumn smiled although she'd heard a variation of every pig joke told since the beginning of time. She continued smiling as she wrote up a receipt for a full-page advertisement and handed it to Maria just as the door squeaked open.

"Morning." Clay removed his hat.

"And another eager client." Maria smiled knowingly. "I'll go get your files." She bustled down the hallway.

The phone rang, and as the receptionist answered it, Autumn turned to Clay. "Good news. Yellow Rose Matchmakers just took out a full-page advertisement in the program.'' Autumn smiled in triumph and tucked the order form into her portfolio.

"Congratulations. I was just on the phone with Garcia and Delgado.''

"The advertising agency?''

Clay nodded. "They're talking about donating the layout for the program. I'm going to meet with them right after I finish up here.''

"That's…wonderful.'' It *was* wonderful. After all, they were both working toward the same goal. The more money they brought in, the more there would be in the auction pool for the kids. It was just that the donation would be even more wonderful if it had been credited to Autumn's Hogs and Kisses instead of Clay's High on the Hog.

"Here we are,'' Maria said, returning, and gave them each a packet.

"There, uh, wasn't any trouble, was there?'' Clay asked.

"What kind of trouble were you expectin'?''

"Well…you were able to find three matches?''

Maria pursed her lips and flapped her hands at him. "We found a lotta matches. These are the best three for you.'' She tapped the white envelope with her pen. "What do you think? Your future wife could be in there.''

Autumn stared at Clay's envelope, an odd fluttering in her chest. *His future wife.* And she hadn't looked beyond getting a date for the Champion Buyers' Ball.

"There are also evaluation forms for you to fill out after each date. Then, if your initial matches don't work out and you want to be rematched, we can make adjustments on your profiles. Some people say one thing when they want another, you know?''

Clay smiled tightly and whipped out a credit card.

''Thank you, ma'am,'' he said after he'd scrawled his name on the slip. He straightened, folded his receipt and nodded to Autumn. ''Good luck.''

''Yeah.'' She gripped her packet, curiously reluctant to even look at the names inside. ''Same to you.''

It seemed as though he was about to say something else, but he just nodded again, put on his hat and strode out the door.

Autumn watched him continue down the steps.

''You coulda saved a lot of money if you'd just dated him,'' Maria said.

''Why?'' Autumn turned back around. ''We didn't match with each other, did we?''

Maria blinked. ''Did you want to?''

''Well, no. Otherwise, we wouldn't have signed up here.''

''Okay, then.''

''Don't get me wrong. I've known Clay forever.'' Autumn withdrew her checkbook from her purse. ''We grew up next door to each other.''

Maria didn't say anything, which Autumn already figured out was unusual for her.

''Thank you for your contribution,'' Autumn said to cover the awkward silence. ''We'll be sending Yellow Rose Matchmakers two tickets for the Swine Auction Breakfast.'' She tore off her check and handed it to Maria.

''I hope you find what you're looking for,'' Maria said, placing the check in a bank pouch.

What an odd thing to say. Not "I hope one of the matches works for you" or even "Good Luck".

Shaking it off, Autumn tossed the envelope on the seat of her car and drove over to a coffee shop on the River Walk where she was scheduled to meet with the Hogs and Kisses women.

Clay put off opening the envelope until after his meeting with Garcia and Delgado. It was on the pickup's seat waiting for him when he climbed in.

Instead of immediately driving off, he punched on the radio to a country music station and picked up the packet.

For the first time since he could remember, he didn't know what the future held. Of course nobody knew his exact future, but Clay found he could predict the basic details of his life with reasonable accuracy. Money would be short, work would be hard, and Autumn Reese would wander through his thoughts.

He shook his head. He couldn't imagine a life without Autumn getting on his nerves—or with her always getting on his nerves. In fact, he couldn't imagine his life without Autumn in it, the way he couldn't imagine life without the ranch.

He'd been born to it. Four generations of Barnetts had lived on the land, weathered droughts, depression and the ups and downs of the cattle market. For him, the land was a sacred trust.

And Autumn, well… He stared at the Yellow Rose packet. *Your future wife could be in there.* He fingered the envelope, then ripped it open.

There were three sheets with a biographical summary obviously taken from the profiles, along with a name, post office box and telephone number.

So call him shallow, but Clay wished he had a picture. He flipped through the names and realized he was surprised not to have been matched with Autumn.

Each match listed a percentage of probable compatibility. Clay's highest was eighty-four percent, which sounded like a B grade to him. The others were in the seventies. The fact that Autumn hadn't made the cut meant that her profile and his must have had a near-failing percentage of compatibility.

Of course, lately they'd gotten along like oil and water, but not getting matched with her disappointed Clay.

He reshuffled the papers, deciding to call Miss Eighty-four percent, Julia Holbrook. Maybe she was free for dinner tonight.

After the meeting with her Hogs and Kisses committee was over and the women had left, Autumn had a few minutes before she went to her part-time job as a legal clerk for a law firm in downtown San Antonio.

Autumn had always known she would have to have a career or a job of some sort and had worked since she was a teenager. In most ranch families, someone, usually the wife, had to bring in needed cash.

Not at Clay's ranch, though. The Golden B was considerably larger than hers and could support a family.

Not that it mattered to her one way or the other.

Autumn ordered a large double mocha latte, then opened her packet from the Yellow Rose. She quickly scanned the names and became annoyed with herself when she realized she was looking for Clay's.

What were these percentages? Autumn read the explanation, then the one-page bios.

The men sounded interesting. Nothing that pegged her zing meter, but she hadn't seen them yet. Whom to call first?

Autumn found she was a little nervous, so she decided to call match number two so she could practice on him. George Garza had a grade, or rather ''probability percentage'', of eighty-six percent. Number one was ninety-one percent.

Okay. Before she lost her nerve, Autumn used the public pay phone and called the message service, hoping George would suggest getting together. Soon.

FAX
To: Deb
From: Nel
They're going to dinner tonight at Jason's on the River Walk! Chill the champagne!

Giddy with happiness, *N.*

FACSIMILE
To: Nellie Barnett, G B Ranch
From: Debra Reese, R. Ranch
Take the champagne out of the ice bucket. They're going to dinner at Jason's, but not with each other. What happened?

D.

Autumn barely had time to make the hour-and-a-half round trip from her home back into San Antonio after work.

It turned out that George was a high school teacher and tonight was his only free night until Saturday. Since Autumn didn't want to wait nearly a whole week, she agreed to dinner even though she would have preferred an activity of some sort.

George had suggested Jason's, a River Walk restaurant popular with both tourists and locals. Clay's family liked to celebrate birthdays there. It was a pricey restaurant. Since George was her second choice, Autumn felt guilty about the expense and resolved to pay for her own dinner.

She'd decided to wear her red suede jacket and denim skirt because it would be easy for George to spot her. Brown hair and brown eyes weren't distinctive enough by themselves.

Autumn parked in a lot close to the River Walk a few minutes early because she'd driven faster than she should have. She chose to walk on the path down by the river rather than cutting through the shops and hotels that lined the banks.

The main portion of Jason's was on a terrace with a great river view. There was also a downstairs level, then an outdoor bar that was on the river level. This was where she'd agreed to meet George. He'd promised to wear a yellow rose, which she thought was a little hokey but decided not to hold it against him.

Once the sun went down, the air rapidly turned cool, as it always did this time of year. The cantina two doors down featured a Mexican mariachi band, and Autumn leaned against the railing, enjoying the catchy music while she scanned the path for a man who might be George.

Lights twinkled on up and down the river. A river boat floated a load of tourists to the platform below the restaurant. Autumn hoped they weren't planning to eat here. It was too chilly to eat outside, and with that many people the main dining room of the restaurant would be too noisy for conversation.

As she watched, hoping they'd disperse, a tall man cut through them, going against the flow. She liked the way he moved. She couldn't be lucky enough for him to be George, could she? His face was obscured by his black cowboy hat, so she searched his lapel for a yellow rose.

There wasn't one, and she gave a tiny sigh. Still, she watched him. When he reached the bottom of the steps leading to the restaurant bar, he looked up and Autumn found herself staring at his face.

Her heart gave a ka-thump in the split second before her brain recognized him. "Clay?"

"Autumn...what are you doing here?" Clay removed his hat. His light brown hair was slicked back and he was wearing his Sunday boots with a black Western suit, white shirt and bolo tie.

Autumn found her heart still ka-thumping even though she knew who he was, which was ridiculous. "I'm meeting one of my matches here for dinner. Don't tell me you're doing the same."

"Well, sure. A man likes to make a good first impression."

Autumn tried to swallow, but the words bubbled out anyway. "You...don't need a fancy restaurant for that."

He took a step back and squinted. "You sure you're Autumn?"

"Cut it out." She swatted at his arm.

Clay chuckled. "So what's your date like?"

"He's a schoolteacher."

"So's mine."

They looked at each other, then away. The Yellow Rose computer thought their ideal mates were schoolteachers?

As Autumn wondered if there was any significance to this, she stared at the people walking along the river path. Since it was rodeo season, lots of people were dressed in glitzy Western outfits. There was plenty of leather, silver jewelry and rhinestones.

"How will you know your schoolteacher?" Clay asked.

"He'll be wearing a yellow rose."

"Kinda like that fellow over there?" Clay nodded in the opposite direction of where Autumn was looking.

She straightened in time to see a stocky man with a beaming smile approach a blond woman sitting at one of the outdoor tables. She was wearing a burgundy leather jacket.

"I said red suede," Autumn muttered under her breath.

"Maybe she's a friend."

"Men don't look at friends like that." And then she remembered the way he'd looked at her when they'd filled out their profiles. She swallowed.

"Good luck," Clay said.

"You, too." Autumn walked toward the man. "George?" she called.

He looked up, his smile dimming a bit, then he murmured something to the woman.

Autumn held out her hand. "Hi. I'm Autumn."

"George Garza." He shook her hand.

His was moist, but hers was cold, so it evened out. So did their height.

Autumn appealed to her better nature. And she slouched the tiniest bit, knowing Clay was watching.

Within thirty seconds, you'll know if it's a go, or a no go.

She would *not* be shallow. She would not judge this man by his appearance, even though he was obviously mentally comparing her with the blonde in burgundy leather.

Blondes in leather, she scoffed mentally. Couldn't he be any more original than that? Autumn tried to remember if she'd put originality on the part of the profile dealing with "desired characteristics in a partner".

"Well. Here we are." He nodded and looked around.

Autumn may have forgotten to include "originality", but she distinctly remembered putting down "good conversationalist".

Give the guy a break. You're not exactly babbling here yourself.

"It's a good thing you wore the yellow rose." Now that she was close to the flower, she could see it was a silk rose and not a real one. She had a bad feeling about a man who'd bought a permanent yellow rose to identify himself to blind dates.

"I've found it's the easiest way to recognize my

date," he said, and pushed his glasses farther up his nose.

"You sound like you've done this before. This is my first time," Autumn confided, hoping he'd take the lead for the evening.

"Oh, you'll get used to it," George told her.

Autumn did not want to "get used to it".

The breeze off the river had picked up and she shivered. "Shall we go in?" George nodded again, and Autumn was conscious that while she'd been mentally criticizing him, he'd been judging her, as well. She resolved to try harder. "Your bio says that you're a teacher."

"Yes."

"What do you teach?"

"World history."

Okay, he knew the history of the entire world. Plenty of conversation topics to be mined there. They approached the hostess with Autumn feeling a lot better about the evening ahead.

Several couples were waiting on benches in the foyer, and Autumn had already noticed the outside bar filling up with smokers.

"Table for two," George said.

"Do you have a reservation?" the hostess asked.

"No."

Autumn was a little surprised but didn't say anything.

"There'll be a wait." The hostess studied her seating chart, then ran her pencil down the reservation list. "We're booked solid until eight-fifteen. I can put you on the waiting list in case there's a cancellation. Would you like to wait in the bar?"

"No. We'll sit out here." George gave his name, then guided Autumn across the flagstones to one of the wooden benches.

More than an hour wait and he planned to sit it out in the foyer? Autumn was not pleased. She was even less pleased when Clay and his date entered just then.

The woman was a cute little blonde with sparkly blue eyes and dimples, and they already seemed to be hitting it off.

"Barnett, party of two," Clay announced, then leaned down and said something to her.

She clutched his arm as she laughed.

Autumn turned to George. "Do you have a favorite period in history?" she asked determinedly.

"That's a tough question," George said. And he didn't say anything more.

"Have you ever traveled for research?" Autumn heard the shrillness in her voice at the end.

Clay must have heard, as well. Out of the corner of her eye, Autumn saw him turn.

"Glad to see you two hooked up with each other," he said.

"Yes. George wore a rose. Wasn't that clever?" She smiled resolutely.

"Clayton just told me to walk right up to the best-looking rancher I could find and that would be him. And I *did*!" The little blonde sparkled up—way up—at Clay.

He grinned down at her. "Julia, I'd like you to meet Autumn Reese. She's my next-door neighbor."

Autumn and George stood. "This is George

Garza.'' Autumn tried but didn't have a sparkle in her.

She also tried not to compare the two men, but it was difficult when they appeared to be complete physical opposites. Clay was tall and rangy and obviously a man of the outdoors. George was an inch or two taller than Autumn—okay, maybe one, but she was wearing boots—definitely not rangy, and looked like he'd rather be at the library.

''Barnett, party of two, your table is ready.''

Clay looked puzzled. ''Isn't your table ready? You got here before we did.''

Autumn's back molars clamped together.

''I forgot to make reservations,'' George explained.

''Join us. We'll tell them to add two chairs to our table,'' Clay offered.

''Oh, no, we couldn't impose,'' George protested with more animation than Autumn had seen from him.

Let's impose already, Autumn thought. Tomorrow was a workday for her and she wasn't looking forward to the late-night drive home.

''Oh, do join us,'' Julia added. ''These agency first dates can be awkward and it'll be more fun with the four of us.''

Autumn glanced at Clay. It was just a glance, but he immediately went to speak to the waiting hostess.

They knew each other too well, Autumn thought. ''This is so sweet of you,'' she said to Julia.

Julia dimpled.

George frowned. ''It will be crowded.''

Crowded was an understatement. They were practically touching elbows.

Autumn didn't mind, especially since Julia relieved the burden of making conversation with George. Autumn couldn't quite figure him out. He intently studied the menu and appeared to want to avoid interacting.

Clay ordered quesadillas for the group as an appetizer, which made George frown. Many things made George frown, Autumn guessed.

Especially ordering from the menu. When Autumn ate out, she liked to try dishes she wouldn't—or, more accurately, couldn't—cook at home. Fish was one, so she ordered the grilled snapper with mango salsa. Julia played it safe with poblano chicken. Clayton, always trying to support beef consumption, ordered a rib-eye steak.

And George ordered a green salad.

"I believe that lunch should be the main meal of the day," he announced when he handed the menu back to the waiter.

"Then the food at your school cafeteria must be better than the food at ours," Julia said.

Autumn had never dated a man who actually ordered salad for a meal, and she didn't know what to make of it. She eyed his soft middle. He didn't look like a man who ate salads for his meals, either.

"You teach?" George had perked up at Julia's comment.

"Yes. First grade. That's why I have a terrible tendency to talk so much when I'm around adults." She smiled disarmingly.

"First grade is a pivotal year in a child's education," George intoned.

Julia dimpled at him. "I'm so glad to hear you say that. So many people don't realize that and think it's all just cut and paste and recess."

Julia continued to chatter away, even managing to coax long-winded lectures out of George. He wanted the group's complete attention when he spoke, which fortunately wasn't often. In fact, the only communicating Autumn did for a while was silently as she and Clay exchanged looks across the table.

She suddenly had a horrible thought. What if she'd put "good conversationalist" on *his* form by mistake after they'd exchanged with each other?

The more Julia talked, the more Autumn suspected that's what she had done.

She looked at Clay, to find him looking at her.

Julia and George were talking shop, something about paperwork.

Autumn cut her eyes toward Julia, then raised her eyebrows at Clay. *Is she the one?*

Clay looked at the animated blonde, then met Autumn's eyes. *Who knows?*

Autumn made a gesture toward George. *If you're interested, you'd better make a move soon.*

He half smiled. *Like she'd choose him over me.*

Pretty cocky, aren't we?

No brag, just fact.

Autumn smothered a smile. She could practically hear him saying the words. It was a result of knowing him for so long.

He gave her a questioning look. *So what do you think of old George there?*

Biting her lip, Autumn winced.

"That's what comes from putting down 'no sports'," Clay said out loud.

The other two didn't even notice.

After dinner, the waiter brought the bill, discreetly placing it in the center of the table.

George, in the middle of a lecture on how the school board was choking teachers with regulations, ignored it. Julia, hanging on his every word, probably didn't notice it.

Clay flipped open the padded cover, at the same time reaching for his wallet. Scanning the bill, he tossed a credit card on it and put the folder back in the center of the table.

"I spend a minimum of two hours a day dealing with paperwork not directly related to class preparation," George said.

"Oh, I know. It's just terrible." Julia clucked sympathetically.

Purposely bumping George, Autumn reached for her purse. "Let me get my dinner."

George not only didn't protest, he smiled at her for the first time since he'd discovered that she wasn't the blonde in the burgundy leather.

"I've got it." Clay handed the waiter the check.

"Clay…"

He shook his head. She let it drop for now, but she sent a look of pure disgust to George.

Behind his glasses, he blinked owlishly. "What? Did you want dessert?"

"Well, *I* just couldn't eat another mouthful." Julia sent a smile around the table. "This has been so much fun. Clay, I...'' She seemed at a loss for words for the first time that evening.

Don't know anything about you? Autumn filled in silently.

"I'm glad to have met you," Julia said. "Both of you." She sent George a particularly warm look. "And you, too, Autumn."

Yeah, right. "Well, the evening has just flown by." Autumn stood, determined to fly herself. "I've got to get home."

The others also stood, George with obvious reluctance. "Look," he said to Julia, "there's a meeting of the Educators for Reduced Federal Paperwork tomorrow night. Would you like to go with me? We could have coffee afterward."

He was making a date with another woman right in front of her! Autumn's jaw dropped.

"I'd like that." Julia's sparkle was now directed toward George.

"Don't forget your money, honey," Autumn said, and was jabbed in the back by Clay.

She had to bite her tongue all the way to the exit. When they were outside and gathered in an awkward clump, George smiled and said, "Well. Here we are."

Autumn wanted to strangle him.

Autumn had the same look on her face as she did when she missed during calf roping. It never bode well for the calf and it didn't bode well for George.

Clay touched her arm. "Where are you parked?"

"In the east lot," she snapped.

"George, you headed in that direction?"

George pointed over his shoulder. "No, I'm parked on the other side."

"So am I," Julia piped up.

"May I walk you to your car?" George asked eagerly.

Autumn squeaked.

Clay coughed to hide his laughter. "Thanks, George. I'm going in Autumn's direction, so you don't have to worry about her."

"What? Oh." George seemed to recall that he was technically Autumn's date. "Uh, goodbye, then," he said to her. "I'll give you a favorable evaluation." Then with a nod, he turned to Julia.

"You'll—"

Clay slipped his arm around Autumn's waist and hauled her next to him, which cut off the threatened eruption. "Wave bye-bye, Autumn." He lifted his hand.

They watched George and Julia walk down the river path.

"They're not looking at us, Clay."

"Nope. Come on. Let's go home." He slid his arm away, thinking he wouldn't have minded leaving it right where it was. "I can tell you're about to burst."

"Aren't you?"

Clay inhaled. "Mostly I'm relieved."

"Well, I'm sorry we ruined your evening. She seemed…nice."

Clay tried to imagine the next fifty years with Julia and shuddered inwardly. "She talks too much."

"And thank goodness for it. I wasn't getting anywhere with George. And he stuck you for dinner!'' She grabbed for her shoulder bag.

''Autumn, forget it. My treat.''

''Oh, Clay.''

''Donate the money to your program-sales fund, if it makes you feel better.''

She grimaced. ''That means you're so far ahead that this won't make any difference, right?''

He looked down at her and almost hated to answer. ''The ad agency donation was a lucky break.''

''Shoot. I figured as much. Well, congratulations. At least I made you work for the prize.''

Clay stared ahead to the Crockett Street Bridge. Autumn never pouted over defeats. She might get mad at herself but only if she felt she hadn't given her best. The truth was, Autumn was a first-rate competitor. No matter what the field, she raised the level of competition so that winners truly valued their win and the also-rans felt pretty good, too.

She'd crossed her arms in the chilly January night air and Clay suddenly longed for the days when he would've thrown his arm around her shoulders to keep her warm and thought nothing of it.

''You know what I think?''

''What?''

''I think that cheapskate weasel never intended for us to eat dinner.''

''So George forgot to make reservations. Give the guy a break.''

She didn't, not that Clay had expected her to. ''Think about it. When you offered to let us sit at your table, he didn't want to. And he ordered a side salad!''

"Maybe he wasn't hungry."

"I think he planned to spend the evening in the foyer. *He's* the one who suggested Jason's, for Pete's sake. A hamburger would have been fine with me."

Clay decided to throw his arm around her anyway. She didn't pull away but walked in silence with him.

Clay enjoyed the feel of her next to him. It had been a long time. "Was he your top match?"

"No, thank goodness. I was using him for practice. How about Julia?"

"Yep."

"She wasn't so bad. The talking was probably nerves."

"Nerves for two hours? That's one high-strung filly."

"Oh, don't refer to women as horses. You know I can't stand that."

He did, and he'd said it to rankle her. A habit they'd fallen into.

"My number-one match wasn't rated that much higher than George. I hope that's not a bad sign."

"You thinking about calling it quits?"

She pulled back and gave him a look. "No way. Besides, our names are in the database now. Maybe we'll get matched with more people."

"Maybe." But dare or no dare, the thought of Autumn dating a bunch of men right under his nose didn't thrill him.

They cut around the curved stone wall of a garden and climbed the several steps from the river to street level.

Autumn's black Bronco gleamed in the parking-lot lights. Clay watched while she unlocked the door. "How's the gas mileage on this thing?"

"Could be better."

Clay rested his hand on the hood. "You know, I sort of miss your old Buick."

"It was a good car, but its time had come. Passed, actually."

"I remember the night you got that car," he said quietly.

Autumn stilled.

"It was cold and clear, just like tonight."

And he'd been mortified to hear their fathers talking, especially the hormones crack. The truth was, his hormones *were* running a little wild where she was concerned and it had embarrassed him to know that his father had guessed. He should have laughed it off, but back then, he'd been seventeen and hadn't known what to say to her, so he'd said nothing.

He'd been paying for it ever since.

"It is chilly." Autumn drew in a breath and tossed him a brittle smile. "I don't see your truck."

"I'm parked on the other side of Crockett."

"Back there?"

He nodded.

"Hop in and I'll drive you."

Clay did so, more because he wanted to follow Autumn on the drive back than because he minded the walk. She drove right to his pickup.

"Hang on and I'll follow you home," he said before closing the door.

Autumn lowered the window as Clay walked in front of her Bronco. "You don't have to follow me."

He leaned down. "No, but I want to." He slapped the car and got into his truck.

The sight of Clay's headlights in her rearview mirror reminded Autumn of all those drives from San Antonio to Fort Worth and back when they were in college together. Their parents had always insisted on Clay following her and it used to bug Autumn, but Clay took his responsibility for her safety very seriously.

She hadn't been nice to him some of those times. Once, she'd given him a huge thermos of coffee before they'd started out, then hadn't stopped for a restroom break for the whole trip. And, even worse, she'd driven slowly, dragging a three-hour trip into four.

Other times, she'd left without telling him or deliberately turned onto side roads so she'd lose him.

Now, she found the steady sight of his headlights reassuring.

You don't have to follow me.

No, but I want to.

Had he wanted to? Really?

Or was she still just another one of his responsibilities?

YELLOW ROSE MATCHMAKERS MATCH
EVALUATION
NAME OF DATE: *George Garza*
ACTIVITY: *Dinner*
WOULD YOU DATE THIS PERSON AGAIN?
Not in a million years.
WHY OR WHY NOT? *He's a boring weaselly*

cheapskate who should be removed from the Yellow Rose database so other women won't have to suffer through a date with him.
DID YOU FIND ATTRIBUTES OF THIS MATCH THAT ARE INCOMPATIBLE WITH TRAITS YOU DESIRE IN A MATE? BE SPECIFIC. A PERSONALITY PROFILE IS ENCLOSED FOR YOUR REFERENCE. *Easy. He has no personality. Are you sure he filled out a form?*

YELLOW ROSE MATCHMAKERS MATCH EVALUATION
NAME OF DATE: *Julia Holbrook*
ACTIVITY: *Dinner*
WOULD YOU DATE THIS PERSON AGAIN? *Maybe.*
WHY OR WHY NOT? *I don't think she got a fair shake since we hooked up with another couple. Maybe I didn't get a fair shake.*
DID YOU FIND ATTRIBUTES OF THIS MATCH THAT ARE INCOMPATIBLE WITH TRAITS YOU DESIRE IN A MATE? BE SPECIFIC. A PERSONALITY PROFILE IS ENCLOSED FOR YOUR REFERENCE. *She's noisy. Talks a lot. I'd like a woman who knows when to be quiet and who knows what I'm thinking almost before I do. But that's nothing against Julia. It's asking a lot of a woman, and I don't expect that the first time out. A woman would have to know me for years before we could have that kind of a relationship. Never mind.*

CHAPTER FOUR

FAX
To: D. Reese, Reese Ranch
From: N. Barnett, Golden B Ranch
Talk to Autumn and find out why she's
dating other men.

Nellie

FACSIMILE
To: Nellie Barnett, Golden B
From: Debra Reese, Reese Ranch
What do you expect her to do if Clayton is going
to flaunt other women in front of her?

Debra

AUTUMN worked all day on Tuesdays, which meant
her mother had to tend to the morning chores by
herself. To make it up to her, Autumn would make
the coffee and fix breakfast before she left, so the
food would be waiting when her mother was finished.

But when she entered the kitchen this morning,
Autumn found her mother sipping a mug of coffee
as she stared out the kitchen window over the sink.
She had on her work clothes, and the dampness on
the edges of her boots told Autumn she'd already
been outside.

"Couldn't sleep?" Autumn asked.

"I woke up early and didn't feel like staying in

bed.'' Debra sipped her coffee. "How was your date last night?'' She sounded tired and she didn't look at Autumn when she spoke.

"He was pretty awful.'' Autumn told her bits and pieces, hoping they could share a good laugh, but her mother didn't smile.

"Where did you meet him?''

Autumn knew her mother wasn't going to like the answer. "I went to Yellow Rose Matchmakers to ask for a donation, and while I was there, I signed up. Clay did, too,'' she added as though that would make the news more palatable to her mother.

Slowly, Debra turned her head to stare. "Why?''

If Autumn didn't leave within twenty minutes, she risked being late. Driving to San Antonio wasn't the problem—driving through the morning traffic in the city was.

Though people thought of San Antonio as a laid-back village, it was actually a big city, the number-one tourist destination in Texas, with all a city's problems and traffic.

Now was not the time to have this conversation, but Autumn suspected she was going to have it anyway. For the first time in years, it appeared her mother would actually listen—and maybe even believe.

"Clay and I thought it would be a good way to meet other people.''

"Why?'' Debra repeated.

Autumn poured herself a cup of coffee. She was going to have to be blunt. "I'm aware that you and Clay's parents—and everyone else we know—expect us to get married. But we aren't.''

Debra's eyebrows drew together. "Did you two have a fight?"

Maybe it would be the same conversation after all. Autumn poured too much milk into her coffee, then had to heat the mug in the microwave. "No. We were never going to get married. Ever."

"But you love each other."

Autumn muttered and hoped the hum of the microwave kept her mother from hearing. "As a brother and sister, maybe." She ignored the non-brotherly look Clay had given her at the Yellow Rose. And she definitely ignored her nonsisterly response. "We certainly fight like a brother and sister."

"I see." Debra turned back to the window. The gray morning light highlighted the lines in her face and the silver in her hair. For the first time, Autumn noticed that her mother was aging. She was only in her fifties, but the past year without Autumn's father had been difficult for her. Autumn was just noticing how difficult.

The microwave dinged. Autumn retrieved her cup.

"And Clayton feels this way, too?"

Why did it matter how Clay felt? *She* felt that way. Wasn't that enough? "I don't know how Clay feels."

Hope lit her mother's eyes. "Then you should talk with him."

"No!" Autumn set the mug on the counter before she could hurl it across the room. "I don't want to talk with Clay. There's nothing to talk about! Why can't you understand that? I don't know who started the idea that Clay and I were going to get married, but it didn't come from us." Years of frustration bubbled over. "Do you have any idea how aggravating it is to be asked about our plans all the time? To be paired up all the time? And nobody listens when I tell them we aren't getting married. It's like it's already been decided for us and we have no choice at all. Well, Mom, *I* want a choice."

During Autumn's ranting, her mother had silently stared out the window. "Sometimes," she said slowly, "life chooses for us."

She was thinking about Autumn's father. Autumn walked over to the sink and gave her mother a hug. "I'm sorry, Mom."

"No, I'm sorry. No one meant to pressure you into marrying Clay. We all just thought…" Debra's voice trailed off and she patted Autumn's arm. "So tell me about Clay's date."

Autumn told her about the vivacious Julia. "But Clay thinks she talks too much."

"She was probably nervous. I'm sure she'll calm down on future dates."

"He won't be dating her anymore."

"Really? She sounds quite nice from the way you described her."

Autumn downed the rest of her coffee. No time for breakfast. "She probably is nice. But she's not right for Clay."

"Well, I'm sure he'll find someone." Debra cocked her head to one side. "You know, I think that sweet Jackie Dutton has always had a crush on Clayton."

"Clay and Jackie Dutton?" Autumn tried to pair the two up in her mind. It was true that at the New

Year's Day meeting, Jackie had admired Clay's... "I don't *think* so."

"And why not?"

"Because...because she isn't right for him, that's why."

Her mother eyed Autumn with an unreadable expression. "I think I'll give her mother a call."

"Mom! Tell me you aren't trying to set Jackie up with Clay?"

"Why, Autumn, what do you care? You've convinced me that you want nothing to do with Clayton, and that now makes him the most eligible bachelor in the area."

The most eligible bachelor in the area was ambushed by his mother with a plate of eggs and hot biscuits.

Nellie Barnett was a petite blonde with the business savvy it took to run what amounted to a family corporation. She was not the cook—unless she was troubled.

Clayton eyed the family breakfast table, which was loaded with slabs of ham and hash browns, as well as the biscuits and eggs.

"I've got pears left from the Fruit of the Month Club. Want one?"

Nellie stood poised with pear and knife, so Clay thought it would be wise to nod yes and have a seat. Nellie finished cutting the pear and poured his coffee, then a cup for herself, sat at the table and studied him.

It was The Look.

Clay dug into his eggs and stared at his plate as he chewed. He was a grown man, and still Nellie's

Look made him uncomfortable even when he hadn't done anything wrong.

As a boy, he'd rushed to confess whatever he'd done that he suspected his mother had found out about. Years later, he'd learned that she sometimes just gave him The Look to see what he'd been up to.

Hardened ranch hands bowed their heads and stared at their boots as they scuffed the dirt when subjected to Nellie's Look.

"Aw, Nellie…" his own father would say, and look chastened.

And his mother would reply, "Let's not discuss it in front of the boy."

Clay figured he was getting The Look now because of his date last night. He risked eye contact and discovered that his mother's face was almost as tight as it had been at Thanksgiving when he'd invited Kristin to visit. That had gone over like a lead balloon.

He swallowed a mouthful of eggs and reached for his coffee. "Aren't you hungry?"

"Not particularly."

Clay forced himself to keep from saying anything more. He drank his coffee and waited.

"I heard you had a date last night," Nellie began at last.

"Yes."

"Does Autumn know?"

"She was there."

His mother's face relaxed. "Oh, so—"

"With her date," Clay added quickly.

Nellie made a disgusted sound. "What do you two think you're doing?"

"Dating."

"Why?"

"The usual reasons people date."

"People date because they're looking for someone to settle down with. You and Autumn have each other."

It was time he faced this assumption head-on. "Now that's where the truth parts company with what everyone thinks. Much as you might wish it so, Autumn and I see it differently."

"And how do you see it?"

"I see that Autumn is not looking in my direction for a husband." The admission caused him a pang, but he'd learned to ignore pangs where Autumn was concerned.

"Have you given her any reason to look in your direction?"

What for? Autumn knew where he was. She'd always known. And it was getting embarrassing for both of them just waiting around until she found someone else. She felt the pressure and he…didn't want to think about it. "Autumn and I want different things out of life. She's going to go back to school, then start practicing law."

"She can do that from here! We…we all thought it was very clever of her to study ranching law. It would've brought in enough income to cover you in the lean years…oh, Clay." Nellie's face crumpled in distress. "It was going to be so perfect."

"I know what you and Autumn's parents wanted, Mom. Now I'd appreciate it if you would just back off." And Clay met her distressed gaze with a Look of his own.

His mother blinked first. Stealing a section of pear from his plate, she asked, "Is she someone we know?"

"Who?"

"The woman you took to dinner last night."

Clay shook his head.

"Then where did you meet her?"

Clay's breakfast was getting cold, but he resigned himself and explained about signing up at the Yellow Rose.

His mother's mouth opened and closed. "And Autumn's date?"

"Missed out," Clay said. He was unable to prevent a grin.

Nellie gave him a speculative look but wisely said nothing more on the subject. "Hurry and finish up. Your father's in the birthing barn and it looks like he's going to have to pull that crossbred heifer."

"I'll go give him a hand." Clay rose immediately, though calf pulling wasn't his favorite activity. He plopped his hat on his head, slipped on an old down vest and went quickly out the door. Jogging across the gravel yard, he was more than happy to escape further conversation with his mother about Autumn.

The Golden B scheduled their spring calving for February and March, with the first-calf heifers being bred early to give them extra time to recover before the next breeding season.

Since later January and early February weather could still have some nasty cold rain, the Golden B had built a barn and pens to house the early calves. One section was designated the delivery ward.

It was here that Clay found his father with the

heifer. Hank Barnett had already secured the cow's head and was washing his arms up to the elbows with disinfectant.

"Need some help?" Clay asked.

"I'm not so old I can't still pull a calf but not so young I wouldn't appreciate a hand," Hank said.

Clay washed up, then handed his father the sterile obstetrical chains. After watching the animal's movements, Hank reached into the cow, attached the chains to the front legs of the calf and adjusted them.

As he worked to dilate the cow, he grunted, "You talk to your mother?"

"Yes."

"And?"

"And what?"

"Son, Ben's been dead for more than a year, and Autumn hasn't gone back to school. What are you two waiting for?"

"Autumn is going back to school this summer."

"Not if she's got a wedding to plan."

"True. But she won't be planning it with me."

Hank looked up at his son. "You're not trying to tell me she turned you down?"

"I never asked her."

"Clayton—"

The cow shifted and drew Hank's attention. He gestured for Clay to bring the calf puller. They braced it against the cow's backside and hooked it up. Hank then began the laborious task of pulling free the calf's front legs, head and shoulders.

Once he'd done so, the rest of the calf followed easily, and soon a curly-haired newborn calf was lying on the straw bedding, steaming in the crisp morning air.

"I'll get the ear tag and record the stats," Clay said.

"Just look at that new life," said his weary father, taking a moment to catch his breath.

"Yeah."

It didn't matter how many times the cycle was repeated, it never failed to bring a sense of serenity to Clay. Ranching was his life, and he considered the land a sacred trust to be worked and maintained and passed down to the next generation.

His father looked at him, and Clay knew he was thinking about the future and wondering why Autumn was no longer a part of it.

"About Autumn..." Clay began. "I know what everyone expected...but it isn't going to happen."

Hank turned to the water spigot. "You sure?"

In his mind, Clay could see Autumn's expression with her brittle smile. If ever there was a don't-touch-me look, that was it. "Pretty much."

"Sorry to hear that." Soaping up, Hank added, "This is gonna change things some."

FAX
To: Debra Reese, R. Ranch
From: N. Barnett, G B Ranch
What happened? How could they both sign up at the Yellow Rose and not be matched together? There must be some mistake. I'm giving the Yellow Rose a call and demanding that they recalculate their forms, or whatever they do to match

people. In the meantime, should we get Clay and Autumn together and talk sense into them?

Nellie

FACSIMILE
To: Nellie
From: Debra
It looks hopeless, but I don't think it is. For now, let's go along with them.

D.

RETURN FAX
To: D.
Are you crazy?

N.

Haven't you ever heard of reverse psychology? P.S. Don't forget Saturday's barbecue and bake sale.

D.

Autumn hated bake sales, especially bake sales that were judged. Her cakes slid apart, her cookies were hard and her piecrust cemented itself to the pan, crumbling like dry mortar when she tried to extract a piece, leaving her as weepy as her meringues.

Forget canning and preserves. People nowadays knew all about botulism.

So she cheated. People expected it. They were relieved. And her mother got to enter twice.

Or she entered chili cook-offs. Put in enough pepper, and tasters couldn't taste anything else, especially if they'd been washing the chili down with beer. But this wasn't a chili cook-off, this was a barbecue, and Autumn had used the same rationale for her barbecue-sauce entry. Lots of peppers ground into a paste with enough molasses, mustard, vinegar and tomato sauce to hold everything together.

Superb.

The thought of actually having a chance to win something other than the consolation prize for her cooking canceled the bake-sale unpleasantness. Oh, sure, she'd dutifully entered her mother's lemon meringue pie with its foot-high meringue, but no one was fooled.

All the Livestock Auction Committees had gathered for this one last chance to make money before the rodeo and livestock show began. It was held outdoors in the parking lot of Freeman Coliseum, where the rodeo would take place next week.

And Autumn was meeting her top-ranked match from the Yellow Rose. Morgan Dooley was an investment banker who'd grown up on a ranch. He sounded articulate on the telephone, so Autumn wasn't anticipating another George Garza disaster.

She'd worn a red embroidered shirt with coordinating black vest, black jeans and a black cowboy hat. It was rodeo wear and subdued by comparison with some of the outfits, but she was working the barbecue-rib booth from two o'clock until four and hadn't wanted to wear anything too dressy.

Morgan was scheduled to meet her at one-thirty at the ticket-hut entrance. They'd planned to wander through the crafts section before going to work in the rib tent.

Autumn was a little early. As she watched the Saturday afternoon crowd go through the turnstiles, she almost—almost—wished for George's yellow rose.

It was a sunny day, fortunately, and neither warm nor cool. A day she would long for during August's relentless heat. Smoke from the grills hung in the air and Autumn knew that after two hours tending ribs, she'd reek of it, but it was a familiar smell. A good smell.

Autumn leaned against the metal fence pole by the entrance gate. Just before one-thirty, a tall woman in a short denim skirt and expensively tooled cowboy boots walked to the other side of the gate and checked her watch before looking back the way she'd come. And there in the hatband of her flint-colored cowboy hat was a yellow rose.

Autumn had a very bad feeling about whom the woman was supposed to meet.

She didn't get to see because just then a man wearing new jeans and a Western jacket with an open-throated shirt approached her. "Autumn?"

"Morgan?"

He whipped off his sunglasses and smiled at her with eyes that looked as though they'd been bleached pale blue by a thousand summer suns. They were striking in the deeply tanned face, though from what he'd said about himself, Autumn didn't think he'd gotten that tan from ranch work.

Still, it was a pleasant face, with smile lines that creased attractively.

"You're the first call I've had from the Yellow Rose in weeks," he confided as they went through the turnstile. "And I must say, it's well worth the wait."

Hmm. A definite possibility. "What happened to your first matches?"

"I dated my first one for three months. By the time I called the others, they weren't available."

Better and better.

So much better that right before they had to report to the booth, Autumn took Morgan by the pie tent to introduce him to her mother.

Debra was as charming as she'd ever been in her life, which surprised Autumn. Not by a flicker of an eyelash did her mother telegraph, *You're betraying Clay*. All Debra's expectations concerning Clay might never have existed. *Clay* might never have existed.

Just before following Morgan out of the tent, Autumn leaned across a table full of apple pies. "Thanks, Mom."

Debra didn't pretend to misunderstand her. "I've learned quite a bit about moving on in the past year. Now, go catch up with that handsome man."

"I'll be working the barbecue ribs for the next couple of hours," Autumn told her, and went to find Morgan.

When they got to their booth, they were given pink-and-white-striped aprons that clashed with Autumn's outfit but coordinated with the pig-shaped pot holders.

"If my mother could see me now," Morgan said with a grin.

For the next hour, they worked side by side at the smokers with other volunteers barbecueing ribs using the twenty-seven sauces entered for judging. Autumn hadn't even tasted her own sauce. She just knew that anything with that many jalapeños in it had to be good.

Morgan, though fifteen years away from the ranching life, fancied himself a backyard barbecueing pro and gave her tips. Autumn was more than glad to surrender her place at the smoker to him. In fact, it was probably better that way. People were picky about how charred they liked their ribs.

Now this was the kind of date Autumn liked. She could get to know Morgan in a relaxed atmosphere. He fit right in with the others in the booth and, oddly, nobody made any "Where's Clay?" cracks.

By three-thirty, they had twenty-seven plates of ribs labeled and waiting for the judges, along with plenty of soda crackers and milk to clear the judges' palates between tastings.

Autumn was feeling pretty darned good about her chances—until the judges came into view. There, among the five people wearing blue badges with attached ribbons bearing the word "JUDGE" in gold, was Clay Barnett.

And on his arm was the woman with the yellow rose in her hatband.

Clay hadn't noticed Autumn standing among the rib chefs, similarly clad in pink-and-white-striped aprons, so she was able to watch him laugh and talk with his date. And there was a lot of laughing and talking, but unlike Julia, this woman didn't babble incessantly—and she certainly didn't take up with another man.

Autumn glanced toward Morgan, who stood beside her, barbecue sauce splattered on his apron. Someone in the crowd recognized him, and he raised his hand and grinned.

Suddenly, Autumn wanted to pull number seventeen from the entries. It didn't matter that the entrants' names were on the bottom of the plate so no one could see; Clay would know her barbecue sauce immediately. He'd give her a hard time and Autumn didn't want to put up with jokes about her cooking today, especially not in front of Morgan.

Standing near the end of the row of tables, Fred Chapman spoke into a bullhorn. "Okay, folks, we're ready for the barbecue judging. After the judges get through, those of you who want to second-guess them can pay ten dollars and eat your fill of ribs. We'll award first, second, third place, and crowd pleaser. But before we get started, how about a round of applause for our cooks?" Fred turned to them as he spoke and apparently just noticed Morgan. "Morgan, you dog, why didn't you tell me you were gonna be here?"

Morgan shouted something back to him, but Autumn wasn't listening. With everyone's attention drawn toward him, she had ceased to be invisible among the pink-and-white stripes. She couldn't help looking at Clay. He met her gaze and nodded briefly in acknowledgment, but maybe he hadn't realized Morgan was her date.

Until Morgan smiled down at her. "I'm rooting for you," he said, and briefly squeezed her shoulder. She smiled back, and he slid his arm lightly around her waist and left it there.

That would pretty much tell Clay the situation, not that he should care one way or the other.

At that moment, his date said something to him, and he had to lean down to hear her. Autumn didn't like the way the woman put her hand on Clay's arm. Oh, well. He'd soon have a mouthful of barbecue ribs. It was hard to whisper sweet nothings while gnawing on a rib.

To Autumn's unease, a line of hungry people trailed the judges under the awning. She looked at the plate of ribs soaked in sauce number seventeen. It was darker and muddier than the other sauces, probably due to the green of the jalapeños. It practically screamed, "Autumn's entry."

She watched as the judges ate from number six and tried to look anxious as though she had a personal stake in whether or not they liked it.

"Now, this is a rib," said one.

Autumn sighed as they made notes.

Okay, it was obvious that number six was too good for Clay to believe it was hers. She'd go for number ten. She stared at Clay, and when their eyes met, she darted a look toward number ten.

When they reached the entry, she widened her eyes and bit her lower lip, smiling when some of the judges licked their fingers.

Clay gave her a surprised look.

Autumn relaxed and the judging panel moved on.

There was a lot of talking and eating and heavy paper-towel consumption. Autumn refilled the soda-cracker bowl and brought it out just as the lead judge picked up a rib from number seventeen's platter. She faltered, then forced herself to walk forward.

As though it happened in slow motion, Autumn watched the judge pick up a rib, eye it thoughtfully, then take a bite. He blinked, then blinked some more. "Dang!" He chewed, but his eyes started watering. "Dang!" he said again. "Whoo, boy." Exhaling, he grabbed for the milk.

With minor variations, his actions were repeated by the other four judges, except for Clay. He reached for a rib, bit into it and hollered, "Autumn!"

She cowered behind the bowl of crackers, but he saw her anyway.

"You did this on purpose!"

Tilting her chin up, she defended her entry. "It's my own recipe."

"No doubt about that." He coughed. "This stuff ought to be used to clean carburetors."

"Hey!" Morgan appeared at her side. "There's no need to be insulting."

"Have you tasted her sauce?"

"No," Morgan said. "But I'm going to as soon as I get a plate." With a murmured word of encouragement, Morgan left to do so.

The lead judge declared a fifteen-minute recess so everyone's taste buds could recover from entry number seventeen.

"My taste buds have been seared off," Clay complained.

"Was it that hot?" his date asked.

Clay touched the back of his hand to his mouth. "Blistering." He gestured to Autumn. "Courtney, this is Autumn. I grew up with her. Courtney is from Garcia and Delgado and will be handling the layout of the auction brochures."

Autumn perked up. "So she's not a Yellow Rose match?"

"Yes, I am, and I recognized Clay's name from the other day even though we didn't meet then." Courtney maneuvered next to him and wrapped her arm loosely around one of Clay's. "So this isn't a *completely* blind date."

"How nice," Autumn said.

Courtney released Clay. "I like hot food. Could I try your sauce?"

"Courtney," Clay warned, "you don't want to do that."

"Sure, I do." She gave Autumn a friendly smile.

If Courtney hadn't been so…nice, Autumn would have gladly fed her a gallon of the stuff. As it was… "It must be pretty bad. Even I haven't tasted it."

"That's because you know better," Clay said.

"Oh, hand me a napkin." Undeterred, Courtney took a rib and bit into it. "Yeah," she said with a grin, "it's like liquid fire, but it's got a great kick." Her eyes watered, but she took another bite anyway. "You know, if you cut back on the jalapeños and mix in another kind of pepper, you'd have a rounder flavor. The consistency is great. I wouldn't change that at all."

Autumn didn't want to like this woman. "But in the meantime, it looks like I've wasted several pounds of ribs."

"Maybe not." Courtney wiped her hands. "It's all in the way you market them. Make eating them a challenge. Let me borrow your pen," she said to Clay. "Do you have some paper?"

Autumn looked around, then tore off some of the butcher paper they'd used to cover the tables.

Courtney sketched a sign that read, "The ribs too hot for ordinary men! Prove you're no ordinary man. Try one!" She stuck the end of the paper under the platter.

"Nobody's gonna fall for that," Clay scoffed just before an old cowboy came by with a plate.

"These the ribs that stopped the judging?" he asked.

Autumn nodded, and he took one.

"Nothin's tickled my taste buds for forty years." He bit into it and smiled. "Oooh, doggie. They's a-ticklin' now." He took two more ribs and proceeded to eat them.

Autumn smiled triumphantly at Clay and gratefully at Courtney.

"Autumn!" Morgan waved her to the end of the tables. "Sorry I didn't get back there," he said when she reached him, "but we've got customers."

For the next several minutes, they sold rib servings. Eventually, the judging continued. Autumn didn't win but she sure didn't mind. Her ribs had attracted more attention than all the winners'. The only thing she did mind was that Clay's date had rescued her pride.

"Hey," Morgan said during a lull, "I'd better get over there if I want to get one of your ribs. I hear they're going fast."

"You don't have to," Autumn said.

"Of course I have to!" Grinning, he headed for the table.

Autumn knew she should man the cash box,

but…they were nearly out of paper plates. It wouldn't do to run out now, would it? She'd just nip around the corner and open a new package. The fact that she could watch Morgan while she did so was entirely incidental.

Morgan put a generous helping of ribs on his plate. As he turned to come back to the sales area, he took his first bite. His face went funny and he spit out the meat. Setting down the plate, he helped himself to the water jug, drinking three cups in quick succession. Still in obvious discomfort, he started eating crackers left over from the judging.

Poor man. Autumn felt guilty until she saw him scrape all but one of the ribs into the trash. As she watched, he used a paper towel to blot as much sauce off the remaining rib as he could, then put it back on his plate.

At that point, Autumn returned to the cash box.

Within moments, Morgan reappeared. "Autumn, honey, you were robbed." He made a show of eating the rest of the de-sauced rib. Two other bones were on his plate. Autumn guessed she was meant to think they were from her entry. "Sure it's spicy, but that's what a good barbecue sauce should be."

She stared, a strained smile on her face as Morgan took a couple more bites before throwing his plate in the trash.

"Glad you enjoyed them."

"Oh, yes, ma'am, I sure did. Too bad I couldn't have eaten more."

YELLOW ROSE MATCHMAKERS MATCH EVALUATION

NAME OF DATE: *Morgan Dooley*
ACTIVITY: *Barbecue cook-off*
WOULD YOU DATE THIS PERSON AGAIN?
No.
WHY OR WHY NOT? *How can I accept a date with a person I can't trust?*
DID YOU FIND ATTRIBUTES OF THIS MATCH THAT ARE INCOMPATIBLE WITH TRAITS YOU DESIRE IN A MATE? BE SPECIFIC. A PERSONALITY PROFILE IS ENCLOSED FOR YOUR REFERENCE. *He lies.*

YELLOW ROSE MATCHMAKERS MATCH EVALUATION
NAME OF DATE: *Courtney Vaughn*
ACTIVITY: *Barbecue and bake sale*
WOULD YOU DATE THIS PERSON AGAIN?
No.
WHY OR WHY NOT? *No sense wasting time when there isn't a future.*
DID YOU FIND ATTRIBUTES OF THIS MATCH THAT ARE INCOMPATIBLE WITH TRAITS YOU DESIRE IN A MATE? BE SPECIFIC. A PERSONALITY PROFILE IS ENCLOSED FOR YOUR REFERENCE. *Her people raise sheep! We'll never see eye to eye. It's like having a different religion.*

CHAPTER FIVE

FACSIMILE
To: Nellie Barnett, Golden B
From: Debra Reese, Reese Ranch
I met Clay's date. She seemed nice. Guess who
Autumn was with? Morgan Dooley, the investment
banker. I've heard a lot about him, and I have to say
none of it was an exaggeration. He's such a charming man, and from all accounts fairly well-off. He
seemed taken with Autumn.

Yours,
Debra

FAX
To: Debra Reese, Reese Ranch
From: Nellie Barnett, Golden B Ranch,
Inc.
Dear Debra,
Yes, we know Morgan. He's an ambitious
young man who would like to get back
into ranching, we hear. So you met
Courtney Vaughn? Isn't she just precious? She grew up on a ranch and is an
advertising account executive. Clay
says she's handling the layout for the
rodeo sales programs. It's reassuring
to know that such an important job is

being handled by someone of such good character.

Yours sincerely,
Nellie

THOUGH Morgan had been a disappointment, Autumn was pleased enough with the generally changed attitude of her mother and the reaction of friends at Saturday's barbecue to accept Clay's offer of a ride to the final auction program sales meeting on Sunday evening.

After all, they were both going to the Hilton on the River Walk. There was no sense wasting gasoline.

The first inkling Autumn had that things were different between them was that Clay parked his truck and knocked on the front door instead of beeping the horn. He opened the passenger door for her, too.

As Autumn got into the truck, she fired the opening salvo in what she expected to be their usual verbal sparring. "Courtney has you trained already, I see."

"I haven't seen her since yesterday," Clay said. She'd thought he'd respond with something like, "I only open doors for ladies."

Autumn watched him as he walked around the truck and got in. Without looking at her, he fastened his seat belt, started the truck, put it in gear and drove off.

"Are you going to see her again?" Autumn knew she shouldn't ask the question, especially since she didn't want to answer the return question about Morgan.

They'd reached the end of her drive and Clay was

checking the road for traffic. His gaze skimmed over her. "Don't see that that's any concern of yours."

What was the matter with him? "I was just trying to make conversation!"

"Were you?"

"Well, yes. What did you think?"

"I think it's been years since we've had a conversation," he said quietly, and turned onto the highway.

Autumn wished she hadn't accepted his offer of a ride. "We talk all the time."

"Trading insults isn't talk."

"If it bothered you, you should have said something."

"And given you more ammunition? Nah."

If this was conversation, Autumn didn't like it. Clay wasn't smiling and he wasn't laughing. He wasn't saying much of anything.

The atmosphere was cold inside the pickup's cab. And quiet, except for the hum of the engine. Autumn thought about turning on the radio, but something held her back.

"Mom's thinking about painting the kitchen." That wasn't much of a conversational topic, either, but it was better than the awful silence.

"Keeping it yellow, or changing colors?"

"She's talking about painting everything, including the cabinets, white. She says white looks stylish." Like Clay would care about such a thing.

And apparently he didn't because he said nothing more.

Autumn tried again. "Mom says your heifers have started calving already."

"The last couple of springs have been so hot we moved the breeding up a cycle. We'll beat out the northern beef and get a better price for our yearlings. Should more than make up for the increased winter feed costs."

Autumn had heard all the arguments about the timing of calving. Clay would know this, but it was a safe subject and more interesting to him than the color of Autumn's kitchen.

But...was ranching all that interested him? Wasn't there anything else they could talk about? There was more than half an hour left of the drive into San Antonio.

"We didn't have to cull this year," he said.

Meaning all the cows he bred would calve. "That's great." Raising cattle was always a precarious business at best. Cows that ate feed and didn't produce calves cost money. Too many, and the ranch would lose money.

Again, this was a fact Autumn had grown up with. Nothing earth-shattering.

"Do you ever think about doing something besides ranching?" she asked impulsively.

He shouldn't have given her a ride. Forty-five minutes each way alone with Autumn was going to drive him nuts.

She'd curled her hair. He liked it when she curled her hair, but then it looked pretty when it was straight or pulled back in a ponytail or hanging from beneath her hat. She didn't curl her hair often, which meant she was probably expecting to see Morgan Dooley tonight.

All the ranchers in the area knew of Morgan, if they didn't know him personally, and he handled a fair number of investment portfolios for them, assuming they had cash to invest.

Morgan wasn't the sort of man he'd expect to sign up with the Yellow Rose, but Clay hadn't considered himself that sort, either. By all accounts, Morgan was a decent guy, for somebody who'd left the ranching business.

He was a city man who probably drove a fancy car and had plenty of money that didn't have to be spent on equipment repair, supplies or replacement stock. If that was the type of man Autumn wanted, then Clay couldn't compete.

He didn't want to compete. And how could he anyway? His life was on the ranch. Autumn either wanted that kind of life for herself, or she didn't. And now she'd asked him if he'd ever considered doing something else. The short answer was "No."

The long answer was "I love the life. I like being close to nature. I like the quiet, I like working with the animals and I like being my own boss."

"So you never felt trapped because your family expected you to stay on the ranch?"

What kind of question was that? "I felt lucky. I believe that caring for the land, the livestock, the hands, and providing beef to help feed people is, well, it's like a sacred trust. It's my responsibility to preserve the integrity of the land for as long as it's on loan to me, and to turn it over to the next generation better than when I got it." He glanced over to see her reaction. "I'd always thought you felt the same way."

A sacred trust. That's what he considered her. Something that was part of the life he accepted without question. She was no more than…than one of his livestock.

That also explained his mood. He was angry with her for not falling in with the grand scheme like a good little sacred trust should. Now he had to go to all the trouble of finding someone else to bring into the sacred trust.

She'd thought he'd felt the same way she did—and by his question, he was telling her he'd thought *she'd* agreed with *him*. What a mess.

Autumn drew a deep breath. "I do like ranching, but I can't stand the thought that my whole life has been planned for me. I might want to do something else."

"Like law?"

She'd originally chosen it just to get away from home, but she found she missed it. "Yes," she said, and felt something click into place. "Yes," she said again.

"So you're definitely going back to school this summer."

"I hate to leave Mom, but I would eventually anyway."

Of course, if she married Clay, she wouldn't go very far, but neither of them mentioned that.

They talked more easily after that, and when they arrived at the Hilton, Autumn had actually coaxed a smile from Clay.

The meeting was more like a festive celebration as each group reported their total program sales and donations.

"Autumn!" One of her Hogs and Kisses group members waved to her excitedly. "I got the Branigan's Bakery chain to make a donation. Look at their ad. 'When you make pigs-in-a-blanket, use Branigan's Bread.' Isn't that cute?"

"Our new total is even cuter." Autumn's heart started beating faster. "We might have a chance at winning."

She was still staring at the paper and trying to remember if Clay had told her how much the advertising-layout donation was worth to his group, when Jackie Dutton approached her.

"Hi, Autumn…could I speak to you a minute?"

Autumn excused herself and followed Jackie over to the edge of the room near the coffeepots.

"Now you know how I hate gossip," Jackie began.

Autumn managed to nod seriously. Gossip was Jackie's middle name.

"There's a rumor going around that…" She laughed uncomfortably. "And my mother spoke to your mother…well, Autumn, I've known you and Clay forever, so I wouldn't want to be accused of… Autumn, you're not helping!"

"What are you talking about?"

Jackie hesitated, then spoke very fast. "Did you and Clay break up?" She held her breath.

Autumn's first impulse was to deny that there had ever been anything *to* break up, but what did it matter now? "Yes," she said firmly. "It's over. Completely. Forever."

Jackie looked stunned.

"You weren't at the barbecue, were you?" Autumn guessed.

Jackie shook her head, her gaze searching the room, probably for Clay. "So he's…free and clear?"

Autumn followed her gaze and saw three women talking to Clay. She couldn't ever remember seeing women cluster around Clay. She squinted. He looked the same as usual. His usual wasn't bad, but she'd never tell him that.

"Well?" Jackie asked, and fluffed her hair.

"Yeah, he's free, but you'd better hur…"

Jackie was already making a beeline for Clay.

Autumn went back to her group and sat at the table, more than a little miffed that men hadn't made a beeline for *her*. She tossed her head. Good thing she still had one more name from the Yellow Rose.

Jackie insinuated herself into the growing number of women surrounding Clay. He said something and she laughed, throwing back her head and touching him on the arm.

Clay didn't appear to mind.

Jaw tight, Autumn forced herself to quit looking, or people would think she was brooding over him.

Getting out her calculator, she went over the donations and advertising requests turned in by her group and busied herself verifying names and addresses and checking other paperwork. In the meantime, her committee members deserted her as soon as the fajita buffet opened.

"May I buy you a drink?" a male voice asked.

Well, it was about time! Smiling, Autumn looked up, words of acceptance on her lips.

Morgan Dooley stood there.

"Oh…hi," she managed, thinking guiltily of the Yellow Rose evaluation form she'd filled out but hadn't sent in yet. "A diet cola would be great."

What was he doing here? Autumn wondered, watching as he went to the cash bar. She glanced around to see if anyone was paying attention to her. People were either in line for food or eating at the tables. Jackie Dutton had superglued herself to Clay and his committee.

If she fluffs her hair once more, I'm going to yank it out by its dark roots.

Autumn blinked. Where had that come from? And why?

If Jackie wanted Clay, then fine. Wonderful. She'd dance at their wedding.

Morgan returned with two drinks and sat at the table.

"I didn't realize you were on one of the committees," Autumn said.

"I'm not—officially anyway." He grinned and sipped his drink.

Then why are you here? Autumn wanted to ask but was afraid she knew the answer. He was here to see her.

She slanted a glance toward Clay, who was still surrounded by his harem.

Later, Autumn told herself that if Clay had been alone, she never would have encouraged Morgan. But he was there, he was attractive, and he was paying attention to her. He charmed the Hogs and Kisses committee women and, well, Autumn was weak. After all, he hadn't actually *lied* about her barbecue sauce—he'd just tried to spare her feelings.

The first guilty pangs of conscience had already set in when the totals of the top five committees were announced.

Fred Chapman took the microphone. "In fifth place, Roll out the Barrow!"

There was applause and excited whispers. The Roll out the Barrow total was less than Autumn's group, so she knew she'd place fourth or better.

"...Swine and Roses!" Then, "...When Pigs Fly! And in second place, Hogs and Kisses!"

Autumn's group screamed. They hadn't overtaken Clay, but they'd done pretty darn good for their first time.

"And the winner, with a total of—"

"Just a minute!" Morgan stood. "I've enjoyed the company of these ladies so much, I'm going to make a donation right here and now. They're winners with me, and I'd like to make them winners in fact."

Autumn's mouth fell open.

"Morgan, we appreciate your generosity, but it's going to have to be..." Fred consulted his notes. "More than $2,672.34 to make a lick of difference."

"Hang on." Morgan reached for his checkbook. Walking toward the podium, he scribbled out a check, ripped it off and handed it to Fred.

"Shoot, Morgan. You sure know how to put your money where your mouth is." He held up the check. "Ladies and gentlemen, I have here a check for five thousand dollars!"

The Hogs and Kisses committee, with the exception of Autumn, screamed and jumped up from their chairs.

Fred shouted into the microphone, "Wait a minute... Clay, do you and High on the Hog want to pass the hat and come up with, what, about twenty-five hundred dollars?''

"Uh, we got twenty-five cents," one of them shouted.

"In that case, second place goes to High on the Hog, and our winner is Hogs and Kisses!"

During the thunderous applause that followed the announcement, Autumn looked at Clay.

He grinned and shook his head, then turned away.

He didn't think she'd *asked* Morgan to do that, did he?

Autumn tried to make her way over to Clay but was waylaid by her ebullient committee who'd collected their brass pig trophy. Then they had to pose for pictures and accept the congratulations of everyone at the meeting.

All through it, Autumn had a feeling of unease. She hadn't wanted to win that way. And she hadn't liked the expression in Morgan's pale blue eyes when he'd caught her gaze.

At last, people began clearing out. Morgan draped an arm across her shoulders. "You ready to go?"

"Yes." She tried to catch Clay's eye and shrug off Morgan's arm at the same time.

"How about we go somewhere for a drink and celebrate this?" He tapped the pig trophy she was carrying.

Autumn was glad she had an excuse to decline. "Thanks, but I rode here with Clay tonight."

"I'll take you home."

She laughed. "I live about forty-five minutes from here. It's too far out of your way."

"It would be my pleasure." He fingered one of her curls. "It would also be my pleasure if you decided you didn't want to make that long drive tonight."

Autumn stepped back. "What do you mean?"

"I mean, I live about five minutes from here, hot lips."

"*Hot lips*?"

Morgan grinned. "That's what they've been calling you since Saturday."

"I assume you realize that they're only referring to my barbecue sauce." Autumn put as much ice into her voice as she could. "Thank you very much for your donation, but it's time for me to find Clay." She turned away.

"Hey!" Morgan grabbed her arm. "I just laid out five grand for you."

"*I* was not for sale." Autumn jerked her arm away.

"I know that." Morgan had lowered his voice to a soothing croon such as one might use on a skittish horse. He'd obviously remembered his ranching background.

But Autumn wasn't falling for it. Morgan had thought to buy her affection. She was revolted.

"I only meant that I wanted to spend some time with you. Come on."

"I don't think so."

He laughed. "This is the way you thank your donors?"

"Your donation entitles you to two tickets to the Swine Auction breakfast—more if you want them—and a full-page ad in our program."

He rocked back on his heels. "You gotta be kidding."

"No," she said firmly, and looked around for Clay. She spotted him by the podium. When were those female vultures going to leave him alone?

"Weeell, okay, if you insist. But at least let me drive you home."

"I—"

"Autumn, you about ready to leave?" Clay stood at her side.

Morgan tried to slide his arm around her. He winked at Clay. "I've just about convinced her to let me take her home."

"Morgan—"

"She came with me," Clay said. "And I'm taking her home."

Morgan cleared his throat and discreetly winked toward the group clustered around the podium. "I'm trying to do you a favor here, Barnett."

Clay might want to go out with someone. Autumn hadn't considered that. She looked at him, trying to read his face. He gazed steadily at her, looking calm, solid and dependable. In other words, the same as always.

Until he turned his gaze to Morgan. "If you want to do me a favor, you could go talk to Jackie Dutton. She was making noises about needing a ride."

Morgan chuckled and scratched the back of his head. "Clay, I think you've misunderstood the situation."

"I understand." Clay's smile was friendly. His eyes were not.

Okay, time-out. They were posturing like a couple of roosters.

"Morgan, really, I do appreciate your donation and the offer of the ride." Autumn gave him a smile to counteract Clay's coolness. "But I'll just let Clay take me home tonight."

Morgan reached out, trying to lace her fingers through his. "Autumn, honey—"

"She's my responsibility and she's coming home with me," Clay stated as Autumn pulled her hand away.

Responsibility? Oh, great.

Clay had made his statement without inflection, but his posture and bearing changed, indicating that he was not prepared to back off. He might have been facing down a horse thief.

She lightly touched his arm. "Let's go, Clay. This pig must be solid brass and it's getting heavy."

Morgan tilted his jaw. "I'd like to talk to Autumn without your bullying her into going home with you."

"You seem to be confused about exactly what your five thousand dollars entitles you to."

"Clay!"

"Ahhh, I get it." Morgan's smile had a patronizing twist to it. "You resent the fact that I can write a check for five grand and you can't."

Oh, no. "Don't be silly, Morgan. Clay, I'm going to the truck." Autumn started for the door but sensed that no one was following her. She slowed her steps, then finally stopped and turned around.

Clay and Morgan were practically touching noses. Morgan's face was ruddy beneath his tan. The few people who'd lingered after the meeting watched avidly.

Pitchers of iced tea were on the serving tables, and Autumn seriously considered dousing them both.

"Clay," she called from the doorway, then left, hoping he'd have enough sense to follow her.

She reached his truck first, then had to wait beside it because the door was locked and she didn't have the key.

No one else emerged from the hotel.

She hoped Morgan and Clay weren't fighting. Visions of Jackie Dutton tending Clay's wounds came to mind, though it was probably Morgan who'd be wounded.

At last, Clay's tall silhouette emerged, and Autumn exhaled in relief when she couldn't see any obvious signs that he'd been fighting.

Without a word, he unlocked her door, jerked it open, then walked around to the driver's side before she got in. His jaw was tight, and he was obviously angry, so Autumn thought she'd let him cool down before she broached this "responsibility" he felt for her.

She settled the winner's pig in her lap and draped the folds of her denim skirt around it, trying to hide the pig's gleam.

They'd reached the outskirts of San Antonio and the road had narrowed before Clay finally said anything.

"I'm getting tired of rescuing you from these messes you always get yourself into."

He was angry with *her*! Autumn's mouth literally opened and closed several times as she considered which part of that ridiculous statement she was going to tear apart first. "*Messes*? I don't get into *messes*."

He drew a breath and gripped the steering wheel. "I don't know what you said to Dooley—"

"I didn't say *anything*!"

"That made him think you'd be—how shall I put this?—*grateful* for his gesture, but he seemed to feel that he had a claim on you."

"I'm not responsible for what he thinks!"

Clay glanced at her. "He now thinks different."

"You—you didn't hit him, did you?"

Clay shook his head. "Felt like it, though."

"That's…men can be so stupid."

"You didn't think it was stupid when you looked around for help."

"I didn't…" But she had, hadn't she? "I could have handled the situation. You didn't need to get all huffy."

"What did you expect me to do?"

"I expected you to leave your harem and drive me home!"

He laughed, which infuriated Autumn.

"For all I knew, you were going to abandon me for Jackie Dutton!"

"I'd never abandon you, Autumn." He used the same tone of voice he'd use to say, "The sun will rise in the east," and it fueled her frustration.

"Right. I'm your responsibility. Part of your sacred trust."

"That's one way of looking at it."

"That's the way *you* look at it," she accused him.

He was very quiet. "I kinda thought that's the way it was."

"Everybody thinks that! But nobody asks me how I feel!"

"So how do you feel?"

"Trapped!"

The word hung between them.

"I don't see why," Clay said at last.

"Because you apparently like having your whole life mapped out for you. I don't."

"Autumn, you've pretty much gone your own way."

She closed her eyes, about to mention the unmentionable—the night when everything changed. "I'm still in school. Afterward, well...you heard our fathers talking that night. I know you did."

He hesitated before admitting, "Yeah, I heard."

He apparently had nothing to add, so Autumn continued. "Ever since, it's been assumed that I, that we..." She gestured.

"And I don't like being taken for granted."

"Neither do I."

"What do you mean?"

"I mean, you want to look around and see if you can find someone you like better, and if not, well then, there's always Clay."

"I have never thought that."

"Haven't you?"

She *had* thought that, she realized. But she wouldn't anymore. "No. But it would be perfectly understandable if I had. You go around talking about responsibility and sacred trusts like I'm...like I'm one of your livestock!"

Clay took his foot off the accelerator. As the

pickup slowed, he steered it to the shoulder of the road.

Autumn looked at the gas gauge, but it was more than half-full. No ominous red lights blinked on the dash. "What are you doing?"

The tires crunched on the gravel and the truck bumped onto the grassy shoulder. "Something I've been wanting to do since I was seventeen years old."

He jammed the gears into park so fast, the truck lurched forward. Autumn reached for the pig to keep it from sliding to the floor.

Clay reached for her.

One of his hands cupped the back of her head and the other gripped her shoulder as he hauled her to him and kissed her. Hard.

No tentative exploration, no gradual buildup, but a flat-out, fully passionate, no-holds-barred kiss.

Clay was kissing her! Surprise held Autumn immobile and was the only emotion she felt at first. She didn't know what to think, but thinking didn't appear to be required of her, which was a good thing.

This was nothing like a first kiss—or a first adult kiss. She and Clay had kissed once before when they were ten and decided it was nothing special.

Things had changed since Autumn was ten.

Clay had changed.

Her initial surprise faded and she was beginning to enjoy the feel of his hand holding her insistently to him, when he broke the kiss as quickly as he'd begun it.

"Clay…" Autumn hardly knew what to say. But he'd only stopped so he could remove his seat belt and shoulder restraint. She heard it slither as it retracted. "Clay...!"

He took full advantage of her open mouth. Autumn felt his tongue meet hers, felt his arms enfold her.

There were times in ranching that called for quick decisions, decisive actions and no second thoughts. Clay had obviously decided to kiss her and was putting everything he had into the kiss. For several minutes, Autumn could only absorb the intensity of it. She was reminded of getting caught in a hard summer shower when she was out in a field with no shelter.

And there was no shelter from Clay's kiss—for either of them. He was revealing a depth of emotion that Autumn had never suspected he was capable of. There was no way this kiss could be mistaken for a kiss between friends, even very good friends.

This was a kiss for lovers.

Clay as a lover? That was...maybe not ridiculous, but certainly not plausib—not something she should rule out until she'd had time to think about it. Oddly, with all the thoughts of marriage over the years, Autumn had not considered Clay as a lover. Even now, she was still frozen with astonishment.

And Clay was apparently determined to melt her.

He'd gentled the initial force of his kiss, pulling her closer to him, nibbling at her still-parted lips with his.

"Autumn," he breathed, "get rid of the pig."

She was still clutching the brass pig on her lap. The headlights of an oncoming vehicle illuminated Clay's face on one side, but it was enough to show the desire in his eyes. This was the Clay who'd looked at her at the Yellow Rose.

Her heart beat faster and she gripped the pig as though it could protect her. But she wasn't sure if she needed protecting more from Clay, or from herself.

As a large truck roared past, it shook the pickup. "I like this pig." Autumn's voice sounded small.

He released her seat belt. "It's going to get in the way when you kiss me."

She swallowed. "But I'm not going to kiss you." She was afraid of what she might feel when she kissed him.

He touched her cheek with a hand that was both gentle and strong. "I kissed you."

She heard the rough vulnerability in his voice. It was true that their kiss had been one-sided, and in all fairness, she shouldn't reject him before she'd at least *tried* kissing him back.

Slowly, Autumn wound her arms around his shoulders, feeling their strength. She lifted her mouth, gently urging him toward her. Their lips barely touched, but hers still tingled from his earlier kiss.

Or…was that a new tingling?

Autumn moved her hand to his neck and drew his head closer to hers, gradually increasing the pressure. Deep within her, she felt the stirrings of a response, like the far-off rumble of a flash flood.

Autumn moved closer. As though from a great distance, she heard the pig hit the floor.

And the flood arrived.

It washed away everything she'd ever thought or

felt about Clay, as well as her common sense. That was the only explanation she had for kissing him with such sudden abandon.

"You're driving me insane," Clay muttered, then kissed her throat. "We've wasted so many years. You're mine. You always have been."

At his words, Autumn's sense of self-preservation kicked in.

That hadn't been a kiss—it had been a branding.

She pushed back, breathing hard. "I'm no-body's."

He was breathing equally hard. "You can't kiss a man like that unless there's some feeling behind it."

Autumn wasn't ready to admit anything. "Did you ever think the feeling might be fear?"

"No."

"Why not? I'm alone in the truck with you out in the middle of nowhere, miles from home and you...you kissed me."

"I thought it was time you were kissed." He brushed his finger across her lips.

"What about what *I* thought?" Autumn demanded, ignoring the way her nerves jumped at his lazy caress.

"You kissed me back."

"Well...well, that's because I didn't have a choice."

"And that is my whole point." Clay reached across for her seat belt and refastened it. "Some things are just meant to be." He looked at her. "Why not stop wasting the time of those poor fellas you were matched with at the Yellow Rose and come to the Buyers' Ball with me?"

"Wasting time?" Autumn thought she would explode. "Oh, so Autumn's played around the pasture enough and it's time to rope her in?"

Clay exhaled heavily. "You *are* the most infuriating woman. When will you see reason?"

"I see that I am still stuck in the middle of nowhere with a bully of a cattleman."

And did Clay apologize? No.

He kissed her again.

CHAPTER SIX

FACSIMILE
To: Nellie Barnett, G B Ranch
From: Debra Reese, R. Ranch
I assume you've heard about last night. What was Clay thinking? You'd better talk to him.

Debra

FAX
To: Debra Reese, Reese Ranch
From: Nellie Barnett, Golden B Ranch
What Clay was thinking was what everyone else is thinking—just why did Morgan Dooley shell out five thousand dollars on behalf of Autumn? Debra, with only Autumn's best interests at heart, I must tell you that there is a name for a woman who can be bought, no matter how high the price.

Cordially, Nellie

CLAY supposed he should feel bad about kissing Autumn, but he didn't.

Sure, she carried on as though she hated him now, but at least she felt something for him. From where he stood, that was an improvement.

He felt like whistling as he strode into the kitchen

for breakfast, but his whistling had never sounded like much and it made the dog howl besides.

As on most mornings, he had a choice of fixing something for himself in the smaller family kitchen or heading out to eat with the hands. Or both, depending on how long a day he planned to put in.

He'd stayed up until three this morning, checking for cows that were acting like they might be ready to calve, and was heading out to relieve the hands who hadn't slept yet.

Later this afternoon, he was fixing to go back into San Antonio to start assembling the pens and building the show stage for the auction. Since everyone volunteering for the rodeo was expected to help, he fully expected Autumn to put in an appearance, as well.

And knowing Autumn, she would be dragging along the poor fellow from the Yellow Rose.

He opened the refrigerator. That was one stubborn female.

He knew she didn't like to be compared to an unbroken colt, but that was how he thought of her. She wasn't ready to submit to the bridle yet.

Eggs. He felt like having a big mess of eggs and hang the cholesterol. And he didn't want Cookie's eggs, which usually had pieces of shell in them that made a person think he'd chipped a tooth.

Well, if Autumn was going to bring someone to the work party, then so was he. After all, she *had* kissed him back, and it was the sweetest kiss he'd ever had, too. He remembered the exact instant when her lips trembled and he'd known she was tapping into the feelings that flowed between them.

It had scared her. Heck, it had scared him at first, too. So he'd let her have this last rebellion because when she'd had a chance to think, he knew she'd see things his way.

On that thought, Clay cracked an egg into the iron skillet.

And then he had to fish out a piece of shell.

"Autumn, people are talking." Debra cleared a place on the bookshelves in the den and set Autumn's brass pig in the spot.

Autumn was on her way through the den to the kitchen for a quick cup of coffee before leaving for work. Anticipating Debra's comment, or a variation of it, she had purposely left too little time for a mother-daughter talk.

She dropped her coat and purse on the chair by the front door. "I'm not surprised. They're probably just jealous that my committee won." Stressing the winning part would appeal to her mother's pride.

"It's the *way* your committee won that they're talking about." Debra stepped back to admire the pig, then pulled a soft cloth from her work apron and wiped at it. "Autumn, did you know there's a dent in the pig?"

Fortunately, her back was to her mother as Autumn walked into the kitchen. She closed her eyes and concentrated on keeping her voice casual. "I dropped it on the floor of Clay's truck."

"Oh, Autumn," her mother fretted. "You should be more careful."

Right. Autumn's hand shook as she poured herself a mug of coffee. Her hands had shaken last night, too. Her whole body had shaken last night. Even her head, where her thoughts had whirled and refused to settle until very late—or very early, depending on the point of view.

"People are wondering just exactly what's between you and Morgan Dooley."

Autumn jumped and spilled her coffee. Her mother had materialized right by her elbow. "Nothing is between me and Morgan Dooley," she said as she dabbed up the spill.

"Just like nothing is between you and Clay?" her mother asked.

Autumn was very glad she was kneeling on the floor and not looking at Debra. "No. Clay and I have f-friendship between us." She stumbled over the word. "Morgan and I have nothing more than an afternoon spent barbecuing ribs."

"And five thousand dollars."

Autumn stood and rinsed out the sponge. "You know what I think? I think Morgan wanted the attention. The sales teams spent all month raising money and having meetings, then he walks in and plops a big old check on the table."

"But it was your table he plopped it on."

"There were eight of us sitting there at the time." Autumn opened the cabinet and looked at the selection of cereals before deciding against eating.

Her mother eyed her closely. "Then why did Clay feel compelled to threaten him?"

"Maybe Clay is a sore loser. Who knows why he does what he does?"

Debra's eyebrows rose.

"Look, Mom, I've got to go into work early today

so I can help set the auction up this afternoon. I won't be home until late."

"Be sure and let Clay follow you home."

"Mother."

"Sorry," her mother said with a faint smile. "It's just a habit."

Autumn dumped her coffee into a travel mug and snapped on the lid. "Why don't you get a ride in with Clay and come help us set up?"

Debra gestured to the kitchen table, which, along with the chairs, was pushed to the side by the bay window. A gallon of white paint was on the counter. "Today is a good day to paint."

Autumn tried to imagine the kitchen white and couldn't. It had been yellow her entire life. "I feel guilty about leaving you to paint by yourself."

Debra smiled one of her all-knowing mother smiles. "If that's all you have to feel guilty about, then go and have a good time."

Her mother must know something had happened. Maybe. It was hard to tell what she was thinking these days. Autumn left for work and considered herself lucky to have made the escape.

All the way into San Antonio, she thought about facing everyone again. Surely Morgan wouldn't be at the work party.

But Clay would.

What was she supposed to say to Clay? After that kiss, Clay wasn't Clay anymore. He was a man—a man who made her very aware that she was a woman. She'd relived their kiss—what she could remember of it—and had tried to make sense of her feelings.

She'd finally decided that she was just surprised and confused. Anyone who'd been kissed senseless would be.

What she had to remember was Clay's arrogance. Yes, he still assumed that she'd eventually marry him, and in the meantime, he was humoring her.

If there was anything Autumn hated, it was being humored.

He assumed too much. He probably thought she'd melt all over him when they saw each other this afternoon. Then he'd gloat about being right. But he wasn't right, and she was going to prove it to him.

Autumn smiled. When she saw Clay this afternoon, it would be on the arm of Yellow Rose match number three.

Garth Rivers was in town for the rodeo and had reactivated his Yellow Rose file. He said he didn't mind the short notice Autumn gave him because he had a year's worth of women to meet in two weeks.

That didn't strike Autumn as being very promising, but she was only looking for someone to send a message to Clay—and Morgan, too, should he be so foolish as to show up.

Garth was one of a group of adults chaperoning the students in San Antonio who were showing their animals at the livestock exhibition. He'd graciously offered to "pound a few nails", then stay on for the catered barbecue afterward. This time of year, Autumn overdosed on barbecue, but it seemed un-Texan not to.

After work, Autumn changed into an older pair of jeans, then drove to the Coliseum. Horse trailers,

livestock trucks and motor homes were already filling the parking lot and would remain there for the
two weeks of the rodeo. She had gotten a map showing the area his group had been assigned. Autumn
parked her Bronco and looked for the license plate
of the motor home Garth was using.

He'd protested her coming to get him, but Autumn
wanted him with her when she went to the meeting
before the actual work began. There was only one
motor home among the horse trailers in section E-4,
and Autumn headed toward it, picking her way over
mud splatters, bits of straw and other animal debris.

She heard a strikingly deep male voice giving
good-natured orders to a group of teens and preteens
as they unloaded their animals.

"Garth!" a girl cried. "He's getting away!"

"Hang on to the rope!"

Autumn saw a potbellied pig try to escape, causing
general laughter. Grinning, she stepped around a
horse trailer and saw the owner of the deep voice
reattaching the lead to the pig.

All Autumn could do was stare. It was as if
Hollywood had collided with the heart of Texas and
Garth was the result.

The man was too handsome to be a cowboy was
Autumn's first thought. Dressed from hat to boots all
in black, with impossibly white teeth, a strong jaw
and a wicked grin, he was a fantasy come to life.

He couldn't be more perfect if he'd been made to
order. This man would dazzle the gossip right out of
the women on the Swine Auction Committee.

Garth patted the pig and stood. One of the youths

said something to him and he glanced over at her. "Autumn Reese?"

She nodded, finding it difficult to speak now that his identity had been confirmed and she realized he was, indeed, match number three.

Eighty percent? Were the people at Yellow Rose nuts? This man should get extra percentage points for just existing.

He turned, and the afternoon sun caught the gleam of a gold rodeo champion belt buckle.

So much for him being too handsome to be a cowboy.

He waved an arm. "Well, c'mon over here."

As Autumn approached, Garth winked broadly at the young males in the group, which caused a lot of elbowing and grinning that she pretended to ignore.

Hands on hips, he looked her up and down. "Howdy, pretty lady."

Autumn felt herself blush when she might have frozen a lesser mortal with a look. "Howdy yourself."

"Hey, ever'body, this here's Autumn," he announced in his west Texas twang. "We're going to be settin' up the swine auction area if anybody needs me. Until I get back, y'all keep your noses clean, y'hear?"

After issuing a couple more instructions, Garth draped a heavy arm across Autumn's shoulders and walked her to the Coliseum. Under other circumstances, Autumn would have objected to his overfamiliarity, but expansive, larger-than-life gestures seemed to be Garth's style, and it couldn't hurt to walk into the meeting accessorized by a handsome cowboy.

The main area of the Coliseum was a hive of activity as pens and walkways were assembled, and trucks unloaded dirt, straw and feed. Autumn and Garth walked near the outer edge and headed for the meeting rooms.

Garth inhaled. "Ain't nothing like the pure smell of fresh, prime livestock and hope." He grinned.

Autumn grinned back, thinking that she'd taken it all for granted lately. "You've been around a lot of livestock shows and rodeos, haven't you?"

"Yep. I was a rodeo cowboy, competing full-time for a couple of years, then I cut back to weekends, but I wasn't winning enough anymore to pay for the travel and entry fees." Then Garth told her a couple of rodeo stories.

Autumn guessed that he was the kind of man who had a thousand stories and had told them at least that many times.

"I barrel raced when I was a teenager," she told him.

"You any good at it?"

"Sure was."

Laughing, he gripped her shoulders. "I like a gal who knows her own worth." And he started in on another story.

She was laughing when they walked through the meeting-room door, but she heard the immediate lull in the conversation as female antennae were raised.

Autumn kept her gaze fixed on Garth—difficult since he was scanning the room as he talked. Autumn didn't want to scan the room. She wanted to pretend

that the presence or absence of one Clayton Barnett
and one Morgan Dooley was of no concern to her.

"Looks like you folks definitely need my help,"
Garth said. "This reminds me of the time I entered
a two-bit rodeo down Brownsville way."

Autumn risked a glance toward the auction area.

The red carpet had already been laid beneath the
padded folding chairs where the serious buyers
would be seated. The rest of the people would sit on
the bleachers already assembled at the back.
Technicians were installing the three television mon-
itors that would be above the auctioneer's platform.
Right now, that platform was no more than large
planks of wood propped against the wall.

Fred Chapman was conferring with the committee
in charge of organizing the volunteers and didn't
look like he was ready to call the meeting to order
any time soon.

Autumn sighed. She should probably introduce
Garth to some people. Reluctantly, she stopped
laughing at Garth's latest story—it hadn't been all
that funny anyway—and looked around the room.

Almost immediately, her gaze collided with Jackie
Dutton's, who took the eye contact as an invitation
to approach Autumn.

"Why, Autumn honey, how *nice* of you to bring
us some extra help." Jackie wrinkled her nose at
Garth. "And such strong arms, too."

"Garth, this is Jackie Dutton from the Junior
Swine Auction Committee. Jackie, this is Garth
Rivers, my date."

Jackie didn't even blink—at least not at Autumn.
"You're not from around here, are you, sugar?"

"Nope. I'm foreman of a little spread up by Throckmorton."

Jackie's approach had opened the floodgates. Autumn's committee found it necessary to greet her and be introduced to Garth. Friends of her mother wanted to chat. Women Autumn had never met introduced themselves.

Through it all, Garth kept his arm around Autumn's shoulders. It was beginning to feel heavy.

Surrounded by women, Garth was obviously in his element. He treated each of them with the same casual charm and quick grin as he did Autumn.

They laughed at his stories. Autumn laughed, too, although she'd heard some of them just minutes before.

She was about ready to give everybody a back-off look when Fred Chapman's voice came rumbling over the PA system. "People, if you'll find a place to park yourselves, we'll get this show on the road." The sound system shrieked and the technicians adjusted the levels.

The group reluctantly dispersed, but not too far. Autumn and Garth sat on the aisle, surrounded on three sides by Garth's new admirers. They used to be part of Clay's harem. Wherever he was, he must be feeling irritated over their defection.

As people took their seats, Autumn looked around, seeking him out. But she didn't see him or Morgan. Instead of feeling relieved, she felt deflated.

"All right, listen up, people," Fred began. "Those of you who've done this before, try to hook up with a rookie and walk them through it. Committee chairmen—c'mon down!"

As a half-dozen men and women lined up in front of the group, there was a movement by the door. Within seconds, every male head in the room had swiveled to the right.

Women's eyes narrowed.

Garth's eyes lit up. "Oooh, doggie. Sally's here. Now the party can start."

Framed in the doorway was a blonde wearing turquoise leather and a shiny red-lipped smile. Around the crown of her matching cowboy hat glittered the tiara entitled to be worn by all past and present rodeo queens.

And on her arm was a grinning Clay.

Jealousy stabbed Autumn's heart before she had time to shield it. She only hoped no one else could tell. She sensed that more than a few pairs of eyes were checking for her reaction.

As she watched, the rodeo queen processed—there was no other word to describe it—to the front row. Along the way, she smiled and waved as if she was on a parade float.

Fred Chapman whipped off his hat. "Clayton, just who have you brought us?"

Clay actually took the microphone from Fred. "I'm pleased to introduce you to Miss Sally McIntyre, 1994 Queen of the Houston Livestock Show and Rodeo and third runner-up for 1995 National Rodeo Queen."

Where had he dug her up? Autumn wondered as people applauded.

"Sally's here to cheer us on…"

"Who *is* he kidding?" the woman behind Autumn grumbled.

"...and help any way she can."

Sally took the microphone. "Hi, y'all!"

She waved as the men chorused, "Hi, Sally," back at her.

"I don't believe this," another woman said.

Wrapping her manicured hands around the microphone, Sally smiled her professional rodeo-queen smile. "I do want to help, so just put me to work!"

"And break one of those nails? I don't think so," Jackie muttered.

Garth stood and cupped his hands around his mouth. "Hey, Sal!" He waved.

"*Garth!*" she squealed, and dropped the microphone as she ran up the aisle to hug Garth. He gave her a huge bear hug and lifted her off her feet.

This was not working out the way Autumn had planned. There were no gorgeous rodeo queens in her smug fantasy. There was a dumbfounded Clay in her fantasy. There was a sexy cowboy in her fantasy. There were jealous women in her fantasy. There was a date to the Champion Buyers' Ball in her fantasy.

There was no humiliation in her fantasy.

Autumn sneaked a look at Clay. He'd pushed his hat back on his head and was watching his rodeo-queen date hug Autumn's rodeo-champion date. Only he didn't know Garth was Autumn's date yet, did he? She slumped behind the woman in front of her.

"Thank you for coming, Ms. McIntyre." Fred was once again in charge of the microphone.

Sally went prancing up to the front and Garth sat back down, a scarlet lipstick smudge on his cheek.

Though she was inclined to leave it there, Autumn

supposed she ought to tell him. Digging in her purse for a tissue, she brought it out only to discover that she was too late. Jackie was kneeling on the chair in front of them, leaning over the back and wiping the smear off Garth's cheek.

At least three other women in the vicinity held tissues in their hands.

"Thank you kindly, ma'am," Garth said with a devilish smile.

Jackie blinked and gripped the back of the chair.

"Fred is announcing the work crews now," Autumn said pointedly.

Nodding, Jackie turned around.

Though Autumn would ordinarily work on the decorations, she decided she'd better stick close to Garth. If she didn't, some other woman certainly would. Since Garth had decided he wanted to lend a hand at assembling the show platform and auctioneer's podium, that's what Autumn volunteered to do, as well.

They made their way to the planks of wood and rolls of green AstroTurf propped against the wall.

Garth propped his fists at his waist. "Now who's going to take charge of this operation?"

"I am," a voice said behind them.

Autumn winced.

Garth turned around and extended his hand. "You're the fella Sally's with. Garth Rivers is the name."

"Clay Barnett."

Autumn slowly turned.

Garth propped his arm across her shoulders and

urged her next to him. "And this pretty lady is Autumn."

Clay's dark eyes met hers. "Autumn and I are old friends."

CHAPTER SEVEN

MEANWHILE back at the ranch...

FACSIMILE
To: Eleanor Barnett
    Chief Financial Officer
    Golden B Ranch, Incorporated
From: Debra A. Reese, Owner
    Reese Ranch
This is to inform you that Reese Ranch will be offered for sale in the open market in thirty days. As per the original terms of sale, Golden B Ranch is hereby notified prior to said offering. Bids must match current market value.

Very truly yours,
Debra A. Reese

FAX
To: Deb
From: Nellie
Oh, Debra, I shouldn't have said what I did about Autumn. I'm so sorry. She's a lovely girl and I know she didn't improperly encourage Morgan. For heaven's sake, there's no need to sell up.

Fondly, Nel

Clay allowed his gaze to dip to the arm Garth had draped around Autumn, then met his eyes. *Treat her right or you'll deal with me*. He made sure Mr. Suave got the message.

Mr. Suave didn't take kindly to messages like that one. His grin widened and he gripped Autumn harder.

Clay looked at her. She had a smile fixed on her face. Who knew how much manhandling she'd put up with to get at him? But that was her call. Eventually, she'd get tired of it when he didn't react. He just had to remember not to.

"I've got the assembly plans here," Clay said, and held up the stapled packet of papers to show the group. "First off, we need to make sure all the parts got taken out of storage, then sort them." He approached the wood and fittings. "Everything is labeled. Let's start checking off the alphabet. Top of the list is floor plank A."

"We've got A through F sitting against the wall here." Garth leaned against the wall, as well, arms crossed over his chest. "How about I start fitting them in the brackets?"

"Hang on." *Show-off*. "What we're working with is three separate structures—the show pen, the auction-officials' platform and the auctioneer's podium. It's easy to mix the parts between them."

"Hey." Garth held both hands palms outward. "You're in charge."

Clay couldn't help looking at Autumn to see what she thought of this yo-yo, but she was sorting through the metal brackets and fittings. "Next set is G through L. Gotta be careful when you assemble those since they're an inch narrower than the first batch.''

"That wasn't too bright," Garth said.

Clay hadn't thought so, either, but felt compelled to defend the unnamed group that had first used the boards. "They're on the upper platform. It was added a couple of years after the show corral."

"Whatever," Garth said.

Clay didn't like his smile. Or his attitude. Or him in general.

Carrying a tray of plastic cups, Sally made her way over to their group just then. "Hey, Clay. Y'all need anything to drink?" She'd appointed herself a hostess of sorts. Clay supposed that was the best thing for her to be doing.

He'd been taken aback when he'd met her, but Sally had cheerfully told him that her beauty intimidated men, so she didn't get asked out much. She liked to have escorts when she attended rodeo events because the men were more comfortable when they knew another man was seeing to her needs.

This was not the role Clay had envisioned for himself, but it was too late to find another date and he had no intention of showing up alone this afternoon.

It was a good thing, too. Where had Autumn dug up that Garth guy? Central casting? Clay also had doubts about the champion's buckle he wore. Probably picked it up in a pawnshop.

And he didn't like the way Garth hovered over Autumn. As Clay watched, Autumn bent over to check a two-by-four. Garth unabashedly studied the rear view and grinned appreciatively.

That was another thing. Clay didn't trust a man who was always smiling.

He took the soft drink from Sally and checked off the two-by-four Autumn had identified. Stopping to drink, he watched the interplay between Sally and Garth. Now those two obviously had a history. He glanced toward Autumn to see if she'd noticed.

She had, but was pretending not to. Clay caught her eye and gestured toward the rolls of AstroTurf. For a moment, he didn't think she'd respond, but she tossed her head in that way she had when she was preparing to do battle over something and stepped over the two-by-fours.

"Did you need me to count these rolls?" she asked, her voice cool. "I see five. There. All done." She turned.

"Autumn."

She blinked. "Yes, Clayton?"

He hated the tone in her voice. "Where did you find that joker—hanging around the stage door?" He'd meant to be unemotional. He'd meant to appear disinterested. He'd meant to let her know that he knew what she was doing and was amused by it.

He'd failed.

"Garth is my third match from the Yellow Rose." She smiled across the room. "I'm probably going to take him to the Champion Buyers' Ball on Saturday night."

Clay had forgotten all about their original reason for signing up at the Yellow Rose, mainly because his reason was so Autumn would come to her senses. He followed her gaze toward Garth and Sally. Garth's belt buckle flashed in the overhead lights.

"I like him a lot," Autumn continued. "He's funny, outgoing and—"

"Isn't someone you can count on to be there when you need him," Clay finished for her.

Autumn glared at him. "You don't even know Garth!"

"I've met a hundred guys just like him. He's in town for the rodeo and he's out for whatever he can get while he's here. When the rodeo is over, he'll be gone. Two days later, he won't even remember your name. I thought you were smarter than that, Autumn." Of course, that was the wrong thing to say, and Clay knew it.

"He's good enough to be a Yellow Rose client!"

"Yeah, he probably smiled his way in with some cheap talk. I'm not saying he won't show his matches a good time, but he's not looking for anything more than that."

Autumn crossed her arms. "Since that's exactly what I want, too, then we'll get along just fine."

"That's not what you want. You want—"

"Don't tell me what I want! I am sick to death of people telling me what I want!"

"You can't convince me you want *him*." Clay couldn't contain his disgust.

She hooked a thumb over her shoulder. "Oh, and you're ready to make a lifelong commitment with Miss Congeniality over there?"

Clay looked at the pretty blonde. There were worse things that could happen. "Sally's all right."

"Excuse me, but someone needs to tell her that the parade is over and it's time to get off the float."

"She's just being friendly." He eyed Autumn. "You could pick up a few pointers from her."

Autumn rolled her eyes. "She's wearing a tiara, Clay."

"So? Your date is wearing a belt buckle big enough to serve a Thanksgiving turkey on."

"Jealous?"

"Heck no. Just pointing out that it's a sorry man who measures his worth by the size of his prize buckle."

"At least he has one."

"I didn't know you measured a man by his belt buckle, either."

"If that's what I want to do, then it's not your concern, Clayton. For your information, there's a lot more to Garth than the size of his buckle."

Clay looked at the black-clad cowboy. "And that would be…?"

Autumn tilted her chin. "I do not have to explain or defend my choice of company to you. I like Garth. I like the way he treats me."

"He treats you like a human prop. Can't the man stand on his own?"

"Speaking of props, it's a sorry man who needs a woman like that to feel important."

"What do you mean 'like that'?"

"Oh, come *on*, Clay."

"Sally's pretty, sure, but she's just an ordinary gal. She can't help it if women are jealous of her."

"I am *not* jealous."

"I never said you were, but it wouldn't hurt for you to be nicer to her."

Autumn blinked twice at him, then she smiled a

wide smile that, curiously, reminded him of Sally's. He wasn't sure if that was a good thing, or not.

"Sure. I'll be nice to Sally. And in turn, you can be friendly to Garth."

He'd rather put on wet boots, but Clay nodded. "Sure 'nuff."

"The rest rooms on this side of the Coliseum are tricky to get to because of all the construction going on. I'll show you a shortcut to the others," Autumn offered when she and Sally were ready for a break.

"Why, thank you—Autumn, is it?"

Autumn gritted her teeth. "Yes."

Retrieving her purse, Sally flashed her smile at the group assembling the show corral. "Autumn and I will be right back. Y'all try not to miss us too much." She wiggled her fingers.

I will be nice. I will be nice. I will be nice, Autumn chanted silently until they were in the corridor. "So where are you from, Sally?"

"Why, right here in San Antonio! Don't tell me you've never heard of Sally's Western Boutique?"

"Of course." The shop was too pricey and too flashy for Autumn but was frequented by country-and-western singers and rodeo queens. "I didn't realize you were *that* Sally."

"I am." She laughed and opened her purse to withdraw a business card.

Autumn glanced at it. There was a crown over the *S* in Sally.

"Are you a former queen?" Sally asked.

Autumn shook her head.

"I didn't think so," she admitted, "but you never

know. Sometimes the small rodeos don't get many entrants, or the sponsor has a niece or a daughter.'' She laughed. "Well, you know. But still, they're a fellow queen and entitled to a ten percent discount.''

I will be nice. I will be nice. I will be nice. "I was a barrel racer," Autumn said, unable to keep from doing so.

"Why, honey, so was I, but it messed up my hair."

"That's why I combed mine afterward," Autumn said dryly.

"Yes, I can tell you don't like to spend much time on primping."

Autumn slanted her a look. "Some of us need to spend more time than others."

They both smiled sugarcoated smiles at each other.

After cutting through the corner of the exhibition space, they reached the rest rooms.

"Such a tiny lounge area," Sally commented, then staked out most of the vanity shelf under the mirror and proceeded to withdraw enough cosmetics and hair-care products from her purse to stock the beauty counter at a midsize drugstore.

Autumn reapplied her lipstick and combed her hair. "So how did you and Garth meet?"

"He's a rascal, isn't he? We were both making the rounds of the rodeo circuit at the same time. I was entering pageants and he was roping and riding broncs."

So he had come by the champion's buckle honestly. Not that she'd paid any attention to Clay's doubts.

"I awarded him his prize money a couple of

times,'' Sally continued as she reapplied mascara. ''Then I helped him spend it.''

I'll bet you did.

''But I want *you* to tell me every little thing about Clay. He says you're as close as a sister to him.''

A sister? A *sister*? She'd sister him. ''Clay and I grew up together—''

''The Barnett ranch is pretty big, isn't it?'' Sally interrupted, and the gleam in her eye was not from colored contact lenses.

''Yes. It's a good size.''

Sally took off her hat and began teasing her hair. ''He's the only son?''

''Yes.''

''Oooh, what a catch.''

''That's what they say.''

''So why hasn't anyone caught him yet?''

Because of me. Autumn knew it was only a matter of time before Jackie, or someone else, told Sally a version of the Autumn-and-Clay story. Then it would look funny if Autumn hadn't said anything. She laughed. ''People assumed we'd end up together, I think, which is ridiculous. Clay has a certain kind of woman in mind, and I am not that woman.''

''What kind of woman is?'' Sally asked, just as Autumn had hoped she would.

The gold digger. ''Clay loves a woman who primps,'' she began.

''*Does* he?'' Sally turned her head to check her hair, then picked up a can of spray.

Autumn had to stand to one side as Sally sprayed her hair. ''Oh, my, yes. For some reason, he thinks if a woman spends hours and hours on her appearance, it shows how much she cares about him. He likes a good-looking woman and doesn't mind how much time and effort it takes for her to look good. Now me? I really don't have time to bother with all that.''

"I think you're very wise.'' Sally began putting her things back into her purse. "I mean, let's be honest. For some women, no matter how much time and effort they put in, it's just not going to help.''

"And the other thing about Clay,'' Autumn continued, surprised she was able to speak, even more surprised she wasn't strangling Sally, "is that he spends so much time alone, working cattle and inspecting fence lines, that the quiet kind of gets to him, you know?''

Sally nodded seriously.

"So when he's with women, he likes the ones who talk a lot. He just revels in the sound of another human voice after all that time spent by himself.''

"Oh, the poor man.'' Sally gripped Autumn's shoulder. "And thank you for telling me all this. I want you to know that the next time you're in Sally's Western Boutique, I'll give you a ten percent discount even though you've never been a rodeo queen.''

"That's very gracious of you,'' Autumn managed.

Sally linked her arm with Autumn's. "Oh, I know.''

Clay reached for one end of corral plank A and Garth reached for the other. They set it in the open area, then went back for plank B.

"I saw you talking to Autumn,'' Garth said.

"Yeah, we're old friends."

"So you've said."

"We grew up next door to each other."

"And you two never…?" Garth raised his eyebrows.

"No!" Clay answered more forcefully than he might have if he hadn't kissed Autumn the way he had.

"Well, why not, if you don't mind my asking?"

Clay dropped his end of the board. He did mind Garth asking. He didn't want Garth getting any ideas where Autumn was concerned. No matter what she said, she hadn't had any experience with slick, opportunistic users like this guy.

"Autumn is a special lady. Now don't get me wrong," he said, "but she's one of those women who likes a man to take charge all the time. You know, the kind who likes you to order for them in restaurants?"

"Yeah," Garth said. "I think that's sweet."

"Well, she's one of those. With her, you've always got to be strong and forceful and make all the decisions, and I've got to tell you, on a ranch the size of the Golden B, we need independent women who can think for themselves."

They picked up another plank. "I guess I understand your point," Garth said. "But you always know where you stand with a dependent woman. No surprises there. If you ask me, a strong-minded woman is a lot of trouble."

"Only if you get crosswise with them," Clay muttered. "Oh, and Autumn loves sports. Why, buy her a big-screen TV with the little picture in the corner so she can watch two channels at once, and she'll be your slave for life.''

"Well, I don't know as I need a slave for *life*." Garth grinned. "But a weekend sure would be nice."

Clay grinned, too. "Make sure you get her to cook for you. She's a whiz in the kitchen."

He almost felt sorry for the guy.

"What are you two handsome men grinning about?"

Sally and Autumn had returned. Clay had been nervous about their going off together, but they were all smiles. He drew his first truly easy breath since they'd left.

"Hey, Sal, Autumn. We were about ready to send out a search party for you," Garth said.

"You've got to allow a girl enough time to comb her hair."

Clay looked at the blond waves, but frankly, Sally looked exactly the same as before.

She walked over to him. "Garth just doesn't understand how long it takes to look good."

"You look great," Clay said, realizing Sally expected some comment, but her expression made it clear that she'd expected something more. What, he didn't know. "Did, ah, you and Autumn get a chance to know each other?"

"Oh, yes. We're such good friends now." Sally waved at Autumn, who was once again under Garth's arm.

"You *are*?" Something wasn't right here.

He stared at Autumn, who in turn wrinkled her nose and wiggled her fingers.

Something definitely wasn't right.

* * *

"Autumn, bring me those brackets and let's get this floor put together. I'm ready for barbecue and we're not eating until this is done."

Autumn set the metal bars over the fittings in the planks, and Garth, armed with an electric screwdriver, screwed them in. In between the whine of the screwdriver, he blathered on about the current basketball season. Autumn knew that San Antonio had a team—the Spurs—but other than that, basketball didn't interest her.

She wouldn't have picked Garth for a fan, either. "Tell me about the time you won your buckle," she said when she could wedge in a comment.

"You don't want to hear about that right now. I'll save that story for dinner."

When there's a bigger audience was Autumn's cynical thought.

She glanced over at Sally and Clay, cheered to see Sally talking a mile a minute and Clay with a pained expression on his face.

"That'll do it." Garth admired their handiwork. "Let's go see how ol' Clay's doing with the base."

The closer they got, the more shrill Sally's voice became. "…and then I was San Angelo Little Miss Rodeo. It was the first time my mama let me wear makeup, and I tell you, it made *all* the difference!"

Autumn smothered a smile. Even though dinner would be an ordeal, it would be worth it.

YELLOW ROSE MATCHMAKERS MATCH
EVALUATION
NAME OF DATE: *Garth Rivers*
ACTIVITY: *Auction work party*

WOULD YOU DATE THIS PERSON AGAIN?
Yes
WHY OR WHY NOT? *He's gorgeous and I'm shallow. So sue me.*
DID YOU FIND ATTRIBUTES OF THIS MATCH THAT ARE INCOMPATIBLE WITH TRAITS YOU DESIRE IN A MATE? BE SPECIFIC. A PERSONALITY PROFILE IS ENCLOSED FOR YOUR REFERENCE. *I'll have to go out with him again before I can answer this part.*

YELLOW ROSE MATCHMAKERS MATCH EVALUATION
NAME OF DATE: *Sally McIntyre*
ACTIVITY: *Auction work party*
WOULD YOU DATE THIS PERSON AGAIN?
I guess so.
WHY OR WHY NOT? *Anybody that pretty deserves a second date.*
DID YOU FIND ATTRIBUTES OF THIS MATCH THAT ARE INCOMPATIBLE WITH TRAITS YOU DESIRE IN A MATE? BE SPECIFIC. A PERSONALITY PROFILE IS ENCLOSED FOR YOUR REFERENCE. *I don't suppose it's fair to compare her with anyone else, so I can't rightly answer this question.*

CHAPTER EIGHT

FACSIMILE
To: Nellie Barnett, Golden B
From: Debra Reese, R. Ranch
Nellie, I'm not selling because of what you said about Autumn, although I do accept your apology. I just finished painting the kitchen. Painting allows a person to think. This ranch was always Ben's dream—or rather his father's. Now that they're both gone, I realized I was keeping things going for Autumn—and she's not interested, not really. And you must know that hiring a foreman made this a losing operation. The ranch is just not big enough, and I don't want to struggle anymore. There's no point. And, too, Nellie, I'm lonely. I want to go live in town.

Fondly,
Debra

FAX
To: Debra Reese, Reese Ranch
From: Nellie Barnett, Golden B Ranch
Oh, Debra! I want to put both Clay and Autumn in a room and bang their heads together! Barring that, I'm calling the Yellow Rose to find out how much it will cost to get them to admit they made a mistake in not matching those two.

N.

SINCE he'd spent so many hours working on the swine auction setup, Garth felt he was entitled to join the group for dinner at the Lucky Lariat, a Texas-style honky-tonk that was crowded with rodeo folk this time of year. This made it easy for Autumn to suggest a second date.

Actually, what had happened was that Garth had announced he would pick her up at seven, as though a second date had already been settled. Since Autumn was already in town for work, she suggested that he meet her at the law-firm office, figuring she could use the extra hours until seven o'clock to make up for the time she'd taken off to volunteer at the rodeo.

She was also relieved that she didn't have to introduce Garth to her mother.

Autumn pulled a volume of case law from the firm's library shelf and brought it to the table where she'd settled in for some uninterrupted, after-hours research before meeting Garth in the lobby.

But instead of looking for rulings in cases similar to the one she was researching, Autumn thought about her mother.

Debra hadn't been acting like herself lately. After painting the kitchen a blinding white, she'd gone through the house and talked about painting other rooms, wallpapering a bathroom and changing the rug in the den. She seemed energetic and happy. Frankly, Autumn had been prepared for long talks concerning Clay, but there hadn't been a single one.

She must have finally convinced her mother that there was no future with Clay.

And then he'd kissed her. It hadn't been fair of him to kiss her—or if he'd been going to, he should have done it a long time ago. At odd moments, Autumn would relive the kiss, like the time when Clay was smiling down at the bubbly Sally, and it was making her cranky.

She should follow her mother's example and move on.

It was in that spirit that Autumn greeted Garth at seven o'clock. She would overlook the distressing tendency to boss her around that he'd developed at the end of their date yesterday. She would carefully maneuver the conversation away from sports.

And she would probably invite him to the Champion Buyers' Ball.

"Hey there, Autumn." Garth, again dressed in black and wearing his belt buckle, greeted her. "You're prettier than a speckled pup." He plopped his arm around her.

Oh, please. "Thank you, Garth." Autumn shrugged off his arm by shaking her keys. "I've got to lock the door."

"I'll do that for you." Before she could protest, he'd snatched the keys.

"Let me. There's a trick to it."

"I got it." He jammed the key in the lock and began pulling at the massive glass door.

"Garth." Autumn removed the key from the lock, repositioned the door and pushed the locking bolts into the pebbled concrete. She knelt and locked those, then stood and locked the higher set of locks.

"I woulda figured it out if you'd given me a chance."

Autumn dropped the keys into her shoulder bag. "It was faster this way."

"Well," he drawled, whipping open the door of a battered pickup truck, "you shouldn't have to worry your pretty little head about that."

Pretty little head? "It's my job."

"Whatever you say, darlin'."

What?

He trotted around the truck and swung himself inside. "You know, I found this sports bar with three big-screens and satellite TV. We'll go there after dinner."

We will not. "It'll be pretty late by then," Autumn answered noncommittally.

"So what are you doing tomorrow night?" he asked.

Autumn scrambled for something to be doing. It didn't even have to be important, but it did have to be done without Garth. She wasn't fast enough.

"How about you invite me to your place and cook me up some dinner?"

Autumn laughed. "I don't cook."

"Sure you do."

"No, I really don't."

He grinned at her. "Well now, I'd like to make up my own mind."

Autumn stared ahead and tried to calculate how many blocks away they were from the Lucky Lariat. Undiluted Garth was straining her patience. "Let me save you some time. Tonight, just mention the words 'Autumn's barbecue sauce' and listen."

"It can't be as bad as that gal's I heard about.

Seems she destroyed the taste buds of half of Bexar County.''

"That would be me," Autumn said.

Garth gave a crack of laughter. "I knew the men down here were wimps." He continued with another of his stories. At least it didn't feature sports.

In an attempt to talk about something else, Autumn managed to work in the fact that she was going to return to law school.

"Why are you gonna do that?" Garth looked surprised.

"To finish my degree."

"When are you going to have time to be a lawyer when you've got a husband, children and all your ranch chores?"

There were a dozen responses Autumn could make, but they all would be pointless. Garth wasn't tuned in to the big picture. "I'll work it out when the time comes," she said dryly.

"You don't want to go to work." Garth's tone felt like a pat on the head. "You're the kind of woman who needs a man to take care of her. Now that I think about it, it's odd that you'd want to study law."

Autumn's eyes narrowed in suspicion. "I don't need a man to take care of me."

He looked at her approvingly. "Aren't you sweet? I know what you're doing. You're trying to make me think you're a strong, independent woman. That's all right, darlin'. You don't have to pretend around me."

"Pretend? What makes you think I'm pretending?"

"You are, aren't you?"

Autumn looked straight at his handsome but clueless profile and spoke out clearly and distinctly. "No."

They stopped at a traffic light and he gazed at her, eyebrows drawn together in puzzlement.

"Who's been talking to you about me?" she asked.

"Your good buddy, Clay."

"And what did my good buddy say?"

The light changed and Garth stomped the accelerator. "That you like a man to take charge."

Autumn thought about that for a minute. Maybe there was truth in that, she thought with some surprise. However… "Garth, there's taking charge and there's being a tyrant. One thing you have to know if we're going to get along is that I hate it when people make decisions for me."

"Gotcha." He didn't seem put out by what she'd said at all, which probably meant he didn't believe her. Autumn was trying to decide if it was worth making the effort to convince him that she was her own woman when he turned his head and nodded toward the street. "I think this is it."

A neon cowboy with a flashing lariat blinked above them. Music, light and smoke spilled out the open doors and windows of a metal-sided building.

"This looks like my kind of place," Garth said as he parked the truck in the graveled parking lot.

Autumn believed him.

When they got inside, they found that smaller tables had been pushed together to form one long table across the length of the back wall. About three-quarters of the committee had already arrived. Clay, Sally and her crown were dancing the Cotton-Eyed

Joe. From the number of men watching, Autumn guessed that Clay wouldn't be dancing with her for much longer.

Suddenly, Garth swept her onto the floor and twirled her around before they began the stomping pattern of the dance. He was such a good and enthusiastic dancer that Autumn forgave him his earlier remarks. And after all, Clay had been the one to misinform him.

She was going to have words with Clay—when Sally stopped talking long enough to breathe.

The dance ended and Sally applauded energetically, barely out of breath. "Why, look, there's Autumn and Garth. Let's go say howdy, and then I'm going to comb my hair and powder my nose."

Finally, Clay thought. Finally, relief from her endless yammering. The fun of being Sally's date and being the envy of the other guys had long ago worn off. He'd decided there was as much hair *in* her head as on it. How a woman like Sally found time to run her own business was beyond him. As far as he could see, she spent most of her time in front of a mirror.

"Hello, you two," Sally sang out when they approached the table. "Oh, look, Clay. They make such a cute couple, don't they?"

Garth grinned and moved his arm, obviously getting ready to drape it over Autumn. To Clay's amusement, she jumped up and grabbed an empty plastic pitcher. "I'm just parched. I'm going to get us some more iced tea."

"You do that, darlin'," Garth said, stretching his

arm over the back of her chair and tapping his fingers in time to the music.

Autumn gave Clay a murderous look when she brushed past.

"Well, pooh. I wonder what's got into her?" Sally stared after Autumn, then shrugged. "I'll be back in a minute. Try not to miss me, sugar."

Clay didn't particularly want to sit with Garth, but at that moment, Garth grinned and stood. Seconds later, he was back on the dance floor with Jackie Dutton.

Clay sat in the wooden chair with relief. He would never look at a smiling rodeo queen in the same way again. Heck, he probably would never look at one again, period.

Rubbing the back of his neck, he absorbed the relative quiet. The band was pretty good, with a fiddler, guitars and a young drummer who stayed on the beat most of the time.

A pitcher of iced tea landed on the table beside his elbow.

"'Lo, Autumn." He dabbed at the splash on his shirt.

"You are lower than a snake's belly, Clayton Barnett."

"Sally was my match!"

Autumn drew a chair over and sat. "I am not talking about that."

Clay didn't ask what she *was* talking about because he figured she was going to tell him anyway.

He was right.

"You have poisoned Garth for me."

"Which did you get tired of first? His smile or his buckle?"

She chewed the inside of her cheek as though she was trying to hide a smile. Clay relaxed, knowing that she wanted to be angry at him more than she actually was angry at him.

"He's been 'little womaning' me all over the place. That was a mean and dirty trick."

Clay moved his eyes in the direction of Sally, who was on her way to the dance floor, trailing men behind her. "And you said nothing to the world's greatest consumer of aerosol hair-care products?"

Autumn's mouth quivered. "She only wants to look nice for you, Clay."

"But must I hear about it in so much detail?"

"You're probably going to."

"In that case—" Clay poured a glass of iced tea and raised it in a toast "—congratulations. You win. There is no way I'm taking her to the Champion Buyers' Ball." He drank his tea, feeling as though a load—a perfumed and lipsticked load—had dropped from his shoulders.

Autumn stared at the ice in her glass, then out at the dance floor where Garth had changed partners three times.

"No," she said. "I can't claim victory because that would mean I'd have to take Garth to the ball. Forget it. My shoulders can't take it."

They watched the dancers and drank their tea in silence. "Well," Clay said at last, hating to break the welcome conversational lull, "we've got two choices. You can either go to the ball with me—call it a ride or whatever—or we can go back to the Yellow Rose and ask for another match.''

"Ride with you?" Autumn inched away from him.

Clay grinned. "Chicken."

"Cautious," she said with a prim set to her mouth. "And rightly so."

Clay remembered when her mouth hadn't been so prim. "And now you're waiting for me to tell you I won't kiss you again?"

They stared at each other. Autumn's eyes grew wide. "Yes," she finally said, watching him.

"Not going to do it."

She blinked. "You're not going to kiss me again?"

He grinned. "I'm not going to tell you I won't."

She stared again, as though seeing him for the first time.

Come on, Autumn. Quit fighting it. If he thought it would do any good, he'd kiss her now. He watched the faint flush darkening her cheeks. He might kiss her now anyway.

She picked up her tea. "Then it's back to the Yellow Rose."

Stubborn woman.

Autumn and Clay drove over to Yellow Rose Matchmakers the next morning and parked their vehicles behind a van labeled Señor Air.

"Between the calving, the rodeo and this dating stuff, I'm running myself ragged," Clay complained as he waited for Autumn to join him at the gate. He opened it and they walked up the stone path. "We've had to hire some more hands. I don't know that moving the calving up a cycle is going to pay off like we'd hoped.''

"I can see the calving and rodeo interfering, but you've taken all your dates to rodeo functions you were going to attend anyway,'' Autumn pointed out as they climbed the steps.

Clay paused at the top of the stairs and looked down at her. "Do you ever consider *not* being right on occasion?''

Autumn smiled, but there was no thrill in being right this time. *I may have made more mistakes along the way than I thought.* And it was possible that a six-foot-one-inch one was standing right beside her.

Now that she'd gotten her way and people had stopped treating them like a couple, Autumn felt...she didn't know how she felt. She probably wasn't used to seeing Clay with other women. It was unsettling, that was it. Certainly not jealousy.

"Don't trip on the cords,'' Maria called to them through the open door of the Yellow Rose. Orange and yellow extension cords trailed out the door. "The air conditioner's broken,'' she explained. "My second brother's boy, Miguel, is working on it now. How's your air-conditioning? He's got a few scratch-and-dent units he can make you a good deal on.''

"It's a little early in the season to worry about air-conditioning,'' Clay said.

Maria vigorously shook her head. "There's where you're wrong.''

"Second time today,'' he murmured.

"This is the off-season. You should have your system inspected when the repairmen have got time on their hands. They'll make you a good deal now, when you don't need air-conditioning. Just try getting one to come out when it's August. Even my own relatives won't give me a deal in August.''

"I'll keep that in mind," Clay said.

"So." Maria looked at them. "I can't say I'm surprised to see you two back here."

"Why not?" Autumn asked.

"You kiddin'?" Maria shook her head and gestured for them to follow her.

She went straight to the back room where they'd filled out their initial personality profiles. Leafing through the stack of papers waiting to be filed, she pulled out several sheets.

"Look at these evaluation forms you sent back. 'Her people raise sheep'?" Maria looked over her glasses at Clay.

"It would be an issue between us," he said.

"And you." Maria glanced at Autumn before reading, "'A boring, weaselly cheapskate'? 'He has no personality'?"

"George?" Clay asked.

Autumn nodded.

"I have to tell you, ma'am, she pretty much called that one."

Maria shrugged. "So what about your third matches? You both said you would date them again."

"We did," Autumn acknowledged.

"And?"

Autumn exchanged a look with Clay. "Garth... wanted a little woman he could order around, and I'm not."

"Mmmm." Maria raised her eyebrows and looked at Clay.

"Sally talked too much."

"Yeah, I remember," Maria said. "You don't like talkers." She drew a deep breath and muttered something in Spanish.

"Did you just say, 'There's none so blind as they that won't see'?" Autumn asked, not trusting her Spanish.

"Yes." Maria crossed her arms. "What am I going to do with you two?"

"Give us another match. That's your policy."

Maria threw up her arms and sat at the computer. "And what good will it do, I ask you?"

"What kind of an attitude is that?" Autumn challenged her. "You promised us satisfaction."

"And that's the point. You two are never going to be satisfied."

Clay had remained silent. Autumn looked at him and saw that he was going to be of no help. "We're surely not the only clients of the Yellow Rose with high standards."

"High standards, no. Impossible standards, yes. Sit down." Maria pointed to the uncomfortable plastic chairs. "I'm going to show you something." She keystroked some instructions into the computer, then waited. Moments later, the printer hummed and spit out two sheets. "These are your new matches." Handing a paper to each of them, she sat back.

There was only one name on Autumn's paper— Clayton Barnett, ninety-nine percent. "Hey!" she protested, and heard Clay echo her.

Without asking, she snatched away his paper and

handed him hers. Sure enough, there was her name with ninety-eight percent.

"Why am I only ninety-eight percent?" she asked, sidetracked.

"Probably because I had a hard time reading through all the scratch-outs and eraser smudges on your profile. But ninety-eight, ninety-nine, what's the difference?"

"Why weren't we matched together before?" Clay asked.

"Because I told the computer not to," Maria answered. "I figured that if you had wanted to date each other, you already would have."

Autumn ran a shaky hand through her hair. "There must be a mistake. Please run the program again."

Maria shrugged. Autumn went to stand behind her. As she watched, the program came up with a whole list of people in descending order of probable compatibility. Clay's name was at the top of the list.

It was the same when the program was run for Clay. Autumn's name headed the list.

She felt panicky. "This can't be. Could I fill out a new personality profile?"

"You gonna change personalities?"

"No—but I might answer some questions differently this time."

"Okay, but don't tell anyone I let you do this." Maria put Autumn's profile on the monitor and got up from the chair.

Autumn changed her desired-mate description to include, "a man who likes new experiences and has goals for his life". She tweaked a few more answers, then indicated that Maria could run the new profile.

"You want to fiddle with yours, too?" Maria asked Clay.

"No, ma'am. I'm the same person I was last week."

"Good."

Maria ran the program again.

Once again, Autumn was Clay's match, and she'd increased her probable compatibility to ninety-nine percent.

Autumn's match was Clay—one hundred percent. "No!" She backed away from the computer. "There's got to be a mistake. This is awful!"

Then she caught Clay's expression. He was stone-faced, which was the expression he used when he wanted to hide his emotions. She'd hurt his feelings.

"Oh, Clay, I didn't mean that the way it sounded."

"Didn't you?"

"No. I was surprised and my mouth ran away with me. But I put that I wanted a mate who liked new experiences and had goals."

"I have goals," Clay said quietly. "You might not agree with them, but I do have them. As for new experiences, I like new experiences, Autumn. I want to travel and visit ranches and farms in other parts of the country. Even the world. I like going to ranching conferences and exhibitions. I like studying new ranching methods. We've all got to keep experiencing new things no matter what we choose to do in life. That's how we learn to adapt and survive. The only reason the Golden B has lasted four generations is because we've changed with the times. If you don't know what the changes are, then you can't make them work for you.''

It was probably the most words he'd ever spoken at one time.

She looked at the man standing next to her, the man she'd grown up with, fought with and tried to get away from her whole life. And she didn't know him at all. ''I—I had no idea.''

''I know.''

''Oh, Clay…''

''If you ask me, not that anybody did, but they would have if they'd been smart…if you ask me, now's a good time to kiss her.'' Maria gave Clay a meaningful look.

''I don't—'' Autumn began.

''With all due respect, I don't need courting hints from you, ma'am.''

''With all due respect, if you didn't need a hint, or two, you wouldn't be standing here now.''

Clay nodded slowly. ''Good point.''

Without warning, Autumn found herself in his arms. They were strong arms and they held her tight as though he was afraid she'd run off.

He kissed her with every bit as much passion as he had when they were parked in his truck by the side of the road. She was learning that he held nothing back, kept nothing of the way he felt hidden from her in his kisses. Into them, he poured his dreams and his desires.

He revealed everything.

Autumn struggled and he let her go instantly, a wounded expression on his face, but she only wanted

to free her arms so she could wrap them around him.
Which she did.

And then she kissed him back.

It felt right to be in Clay's arms and she tried to
tell him so without words.

She must have done a pretty good job because he
was the one who broke their kiss with a shaky smile.
"I guess this means you'll come to the ball with
me."

Autumn smiled back. "I guess it does."

Soft sobs caught their attention. Maria sat at the
computer, crying quietly. "You see?" She ripped a
tissue out of the flowered dispenser. "Now go." She
waved the tissue at them. "I tell you, I'm getting too
old for this business. My nerves can't take it." She
dabbed her eyes. "I'm gonna have to call my cousin
Sophia's daughter, Maria. She was named after me.
She's a doctor."

Clay took Autumn's hand. In a daze, she followed
him to the front door.

"Wait!" Maria came running after them.
Reaching the foyer, she took the bouquet of yellow
roses from the vase and wrapped computer paper
around the wet stems. "All our successful matches
get yellow roses." She handed the makeshift bouquet
to Autumn.

"But we're not...we haven't..." She looked to
Clay for help, but he just smiled at her.

"Honey." Maria wrapped Autumn's hands around
the bouquet. "Trust me. He's the one."

CHAPTER NINE

FAX
To: Debra
From: Nellie
THEY'RE GOING TO THE BUYERS' BALL
TOGETHER!!!!!!!! Clay has told me
NOTHING! Sons never tell you anything.
What's going on?

Desperate for info, Nellie

FACSIMILE
To: NElie
Fr: D.
Tlk later. Autumn wants me to helper choos dress
now.

D.

AUTUMN found her mother in the office sending a
fax. "I thought you said you weren't busy."

"I'm not." The fax machine beeped. "There."
Debra smiled. "All done. Now, what have you got?"

Autumn held up three dresses. One was new, but
the others had only been worn once. She couldn't
believe she was making such a big deal out of what
she was going to wear.

It was only Clay, she kept telling herself.

It was Clay, her heart beat in response.

"Oh, Autumn, Autumn." Debra immediately took

152

the pink taffeta dress and tossed it on the swivel chair. "That was Rae Ann's bridesmaid's dress."

"I was going to take off the bows."

Debra shook her head. "Everyone will recognize it."

"Okay." Autumn hadn't seriously considered wearing pink taffeta anyway. "How about this one?" She held up a clingy knit black dress that she'd just bought. It looked sophisticated, if subdued. The other dress was red with silver beading and had a long slit up the thigh.

"You wore the beaded one last year, didn't you?" Debra tapped her chin.

"Yes." It had been her first time to attend the Buyers' Ball and Autumn had wanted to be noticed. Under ordinary circumstances, a dress like that would get a woman noticed. But the Buyers' Ball was the social highlight of the rodeo season and all the women were beaded and spangled.

Debra turned her attention to the unprepossessing black dress. "It needs a little more oomph, doesn't it?"

"I think the oomph comes from the person who wears it."

"Mmm. How oomphy are you feeling?"

Autumn stared at the dress. "I don't know."

"Go put it on," Debra instructed her.

Autumn was surprised her mother hadn't gone for the beads. The truth was, she was feeling a little funny about this dress. It revealed more than she was used to revealing, and she missed the weight of the beads. Still... Autumn twisted from side to side in front of the full-length mirror behind her bedroom door. She looked pretty good.

Holding her breath and her stomach both, she went back to the ranch office. "Mom?"

Debra took off her glasses and stared.

"It's not too…you know." Autumn gestured. "Is it?"

"Yes, it is," her mother said firmly. "That's why you're going to wear it. There's not a woman alive who wouldn't wear that dress if she could."

FACSIMILE
To: Nellie B.
From: Debra R.
NOW you may chill champagne. Clayton doesn't stand a chance.

Deb

It wasn't until Autumn handed her velvet jacket to the hotel coat-check girl that Clay realized he was in trouble. He'd planned to stay casual and low-key this evening, but the woman who slipped the receipt into her purse bore no resemblance to the Autumn Reese he'd grown up with.

Clay couldn't swallow. He couldn't breathe. He'd gone hot and cold at the same time. "Autumn?" he tried to say, but his voice cracked.

She looked down at herself and plucked at the folds of her neckline. "It's not too plain, is it?"

"No," he whispered, and shook his head in case she hadn't heard.

What the heck kind of neckline was that anyway? It didn't stay in one place but moved when she did.

And it didn't seem possible that those itty-bitty straps would hold up an entire dress.

A steady stream of people flowed around them. Clay was very much aware that Autumn had drawn second looks from a number of his friends. Yeah, he couldn't believe it was Autumn, either.

Barely trusting himself to touch her, he took her elbow and steered her toward the public telephones behind the coat check and next to the ladies' lounge.

She looked behind them. "The ballroom is that way, isn't it?"

"Yes, but you're going to have to fix your lipstick before we go in."

"Is it smudged?"

"Not yet."

Her face softened as she understood.

"Have I ever told you you're beautiful?" he asked.

"Not in so many words."

"You are." He exhaled. "You look beautiful tonight. But you're also beautiful to me when you're riding a horse and yelling at cattle, or pouring coffee during a rainstorm and your hair is all wet, but you smile anyway."

"Clay." She touched his cheek. "You're going to make me cry."

"I don't want to do that. I'd rather kiss you." Clay skimmed his hands down her back and settled them at her waist. Whatever material this dress was made of, it sure beat denim jeans and a cotton shirt.

She looped her arms around his neck. "Then why don't you?"

"Because something happens to me when I kiss you. I forget where I am and everything else."

"I'll remind you," she said, and lifted her lips to his.

Why he hadn't kissed Autumn years ago would probably remain one of the mysteries of his life. Maybe that's why it felt like he was making up for lost time.

He tried to tell her so many things when he kissed her because it was the only time she listened to him. They belonged together. He knew it in his soul and he wanted her to acknowledge it, too. But she would have to realize it all by herself. If there was one thing he'd learned about Autumn, it was that she had a mind of her own.

So now, even though she responded to his kisses, he knew it was far too soon to tell her his feelings—with words anyway. Autumn still got skittish whenever anyone mentioned the future, so Clay knew he'd have to be patient a while longer.

But in the meantime, he could enjoy kissing her, couldn't he?

He remembered that cold night when they'd overheard their fathers talking. He'd been mooning about Autumn for some time but hadn't found the right way to tell her he wanted to be more than pals.

And so he'd talked to his father as they'd worked cattle. They'd always talked about the future of the Golden B, and Autumn had become a part of that future. It had worked out so neatly, too. Autumn's grandfather had bought the piece of land that was now Reese Ranch from the Golden B back when they were strapped for cash. Autumn didn't have any brothers or sisters, so if she and Clay married, eventually Reese Ranch would return to the Golden B.

Clay should have known his parents would talk to Autumn's parents. They were good friends. But it was unfortunate that he and Autumn happened to overhear that one conversation. He remembered the total astonishment on her face, and he'd known at once that she'd never thought of him as a boyfriend.

Embarrassed, he hadn't said anything.

Life might have been different if he'd kissed her.

Thinking of what might have been, Clay pulled her closer to him now. Autumn's tongue met his and he flinched at the jolt to his senses. Moving his hand up her back, he encountered the bare skin above her dress.

Autumn's skin, smooth and flowery smelling. Autumn.

Cool air puffed on his heated skin. Another perfume mingled with Autumn's sweet scent and overpowered it.

"Well, look at you two!"

They jerked apart. Clay struggled to remember where he was and tried to focus on the beaded apparition that had just exited the ladies' lounge.

Sally wagged her finger. "Didn't your mothers ever tell you about PDA?"

"PDA?" Autumn asked.

She look dazed herself, Clay noted with gratification.

Sally opened her red satin purse. "Public display of affection." Taking a tissue from her purse, she proceeded to wipe Clay's mouth.

He took the tissue from her and finished the job.

"Autumn, honey—" Sally lowered her voice, which for her meant she was speaking in normal tones "—you might want to go touch up your lipstick."

Nodding, Autumn disappeared into the ladies' lounge.

Sally watched her, looking puzzled. "Her dress doesn't have a single bead on it."

"I like it," Clay said.

"That's because you're sweet." Sally patted his arm. "And I want you to know that I'm aware I intimidated you, but you're not to feel the slightest bit awkward."

"Intimidated?"

"Yes. You hardly said a word when you were with me. But I understand. It takes a certain kind of man to be a rodeo queen's escort."

Autumn stared at herself in the mirror.

She didn't look any different. But her whole life had changed. Or had it?

How could she have spent all this time trying to get away from Clay only to find out he was what she'd been searching for all along?

And what about Clay? What did he feel? He certainly didn't kiss like a man who was going through the motions to please his parents—not that she intended to discount those motions in any way.

Was she in love with him?

Was he in love with her?

Why had everyone, including a computer, seen what they couldn't?

And what about the little speech he'd given at the

Yellow Rose? How could she have known him so well, yet not known him at all?

Autumn was so confused—except about one thing. If she didn't stop staring at herself in the mirror and get back out there, Sally would waltz off with Clay.

Autumn pushed open the door to the lounge in time to see Sally wiggle her fingers and walk away in a flash of red and silver. A familiar red and silver. An *identical* red and silver.

Autumn's other dress. She hadn't noticed it before.

The realization that she'd almost appeared at the ball dressed identically to Sally made Autumn's knees wobbly. Or it could have been the residual effect of Clay's kiss. In any event, it gave her a good excuse to cling to him and he didn't seem to mind.

They walked down the hallway toward the grand ballroom. Autumn prepared herself for people's reactions when they saw her with Clay, but no one appeared to be the least bit surprised.

They entered the room, which was decorated with a profusion of pink, black and white balloons and pink carnations. Anchoring the area off the dance floor was a huge pig ice sculpture and a display of trophies with the names of past purchasers of rodeo livestock grand champions.

The whole idea was to wine and dine the buyers to keep them happy in hopes that they would return this year and bid against each other for the grand champion. Though this ball was sponsored by the Swine Auction Committee, other balls were held for chickens, lambs, cattle and other animals. In addition to the grand champion buyers, all buyers of individual breed champions were also invited.

By virtue of their fund-raising, Autumn and Clay were invited tonight. Autumn had no idea how Sally had wangled an invitation.

The Croonin' Cowboys Orchestra was already playing to an enthusiastic crowd of dancers. Clay tugged her toward the dance floor. "Dance with me before we get something to eat?"

Autumn melted into his arms. "We haven't danced together since high school."

"There're quite a few things we've missed out on."

Silently, Autumn agreed.

Clay steered her around the room with a rhythmic confidence that she was coming to associate with him. Clay only asserted himself when necessary—not because he had something to prove.

The realization gave Autumn a lot to think about.

As they moved around the room, Autumn noticed something attracting the dancers' attention, then heard a loud "Whoop!" In the center of the floor, shimmying in tight silver leather, was Jackie Dutton. With her was Garth.

He'd added a black jacket to his usual all-black ensemble, but the belt buckle shone brightly.

Autumn and Clay looked at each other and laughed.

When the band took a break, they headed for the pig ice sculpture, took glass plates, filled them with cheese cubes, crackers, tiny egg rolls and quesadillas, then looked for a place to sit down. Clay chose the far corner, away from the music amplifiers.

Good, because Autumn felt they needed to talk. "Clay?" she began when they were seated.

"Hmm?"

"Did you...I mean, after we've spent the past two weeks dating other people, didn't you think there would be more of a reaction to our being back together?"

"It's old news."

"Not to me."

He laughed. "I don't know about your mother, but mine's been faxing the entire world—probably with instructions to ignore us."

It figured. "I wonder what they've been saying."

"Who knows?" He stood. "How about a milk punch?"

Autumn nodded. "With nutmeg."

Clay frowned. "Can't stand the stuff."

"Then how come the computer said you were one hundred percent compatible with me?" she teased.

He grinned. "You were only ninety-nine with me. Must be the nutmeg."

Still smiling, he strode toward the bar.

Autumn watched him, deliberately thinking about what it would be like to spend the rest of her life with him. For the first time, the thought didn't evoke the trapped feeling she usually got, but this wasn't surprising after the kisses they'd shared.

However, she reflected as he stopped and spoke to Jackie Dutton, it wasn't just her decision. Autumn was suddenly very much aware that Clay had made no references to a future life together. Was she the one making all the assumptions? Clay hadn't acted the slightest bit territorial where she was concerned.

Uncertain of him for the first time, she watched his progress toward the bar, watched him chat to the people around him as he waited, then watched as he made his way back. She could object to nothing about his behavior. He wasn't smothering her as Garth had, ignoring her as George had or making assumptions as Morgan had.

So what was her problem?

Clay put the glasses on the table and took a seat. "What's that look on your face?"

Autumn had a feeling it was uncertainty, but she wasn't going to tell him that. "I've been thinking about the way we were matched by the Yellow Rose."

"Pretty slick, huh?"

She stared at the nutmeg floating on top of her milk punch. "I always thought we wanted different things out of life."

Clay settled in his chair. "Well, Autumn, you know what I want, but I've never been sure about you."

She met his steady gaze. "I haven't been sure about me, either," she confessed. "I guess what I've always wanted was the freedom to explore what's out in the world and to make my own choices about them."

He raised his glass to her. "And so you have."

"Not really. The choices I've made so far have been so I could get away from here."

"I see." A bleakness settled over his features.

"No, you don't." She leaned forward. "I did it so you'd have a choice, too."

He looked solemnly at her. "I had a choice, but I made it a while ago."

"Did you?"

"Yeah." He downed the rest of his drink. "I chose the ranch and I don't want to live there with somebody who feels like she was forced into something."

"You don't want to live with somebody foisted off on you, either."

"Is that what you think? That you're some kind of charity case that I have to take in?"

Not charity, but he had the general gist, so Autumn nodded.

A corner of his mouth crept upward. "Am I going to have to kiss you again to convince you that nobody's forcing me to do anything I don't want to do?"

Her own mouth twitched. "Only if you think it will help."

"It'll help me." The look he gave her made her blush, and he laughed.

Honestly, she should be way past the blushing stage with Clay. Maybe it was because her feelings were still new to her.

She was both relieved and disappointed when Clay dropped the subject and started talking about movies, of all things. She'd never talked about movies with him before. He was also interested in hearing about her law studies as they pertained to ranches. "The firm where I'm working part-time now has told me they'll take me on after I graduate. I don't know if I want to go with them, though."

"Why not?"

"They're not big enough." She grinned. "I've got plans."

A shadow crossed his face. "Plans that will take you out of San Antonio?"

"There's more than one law firm in San Antonio," she answered, aware that she hadn't fully answered his question. But maybe that was because she didn't fully know the answer.

She knew one thing, though. She was a hair's breadth away from falling in love with him. Maybe she always had been.

There was a fanfare from the Croonin' Cowboys, and Fred Chapman's voice sounded through the ballroom. "Ladies and gentlemen, may I have your attention, please!"

They turned their chairs around to find Fred at the microphone. Standing next to him, coordinating tiara-crowned hat firmly in place, was Sally.

"We are privileged to have as our guest tonight Miss Sally McIntyre, 1994 Queen of the Houston Livestock Show and Rodeo and third runner-up for the 1995 National Rodeo Queen!"

Applause broke out—polite among the women, more enthusiastic among the men. Clay was somewhere in between, Autumn was pleased to note.

"Sally will be presenting the trophy to last year's buyer of the Grand Champion Barrow, which you'll recall was a duroc shown by Christy Fletcher from La Grange. Put your hands together for Mr. and Mrs. Sid Schwertner!"

There were similar presentations for the Reserve Champion Buyer, and the buyers of the individual breed champions. In each one, Sally presented the trophy, then posed for a picture.

Fred stood off to one side, a besotted smile on his face.

"It takes a certain kind of man to be a rodeo queen's escort," Clay said. "And I'm not that man."

"In that case, remind me to cancel my tiara order."

"You can cancel my buckle order at the same time," he shot back.

They grinned at each other.

Once the trophy presentations were over, the Croonin' Cowboys began another set.

Dancing with Clay was different this time and the evening turned magical for Autumn. He gazed at her with just enough possessiveness to send a signal to any men who might want to cut in but not so much that it annoyed her.

In fact, she liked it. She liked it a lot.

They left before the last dance, wordlessly holding hands all the way out to the car.

Clay had driven her in his parents' Cadillac this evening, and the luxury car insulated them from road noise as they drove home, preserving the magic of the evening for Autumn.

They talked as they'd never talked before. Clay had a philosophical streak Autumn hadn't known about and she surprised him with her ideas for laws that could help preserve the smaller family-owned ranches like hers.

"Thank you for convincing me that we should pay attention to the Yellow Rose computer," she said when they arrived at her home and Clay was walking her to the front door.

"It was my pleasure," he murmured. "I'll call

you tomorrow.'' He caressed her cheek. ''We've got a lot of years to make up for.''

''Yeah,'' Autumn agreed, leaning toward him.

The light was on in the den, and Autumn had no doubt that her mother was waiting up for her. Clay must have suspected it, as well, because his good-night kiss was all too brief.

Thorough, but brief.

But he more than made up for it with his parting words. He took her hands. ''Autumn, I know you've got a lot to think about.'' He shook his head slightly, then corrected himself, ''Several *choices* to make. But while you're making them, I want you to remember that I love you. I always have and I always will.''

CHAPTER TEN

FACSIMILE
To: Debra Reese, Reese Ranch
From: Fred Chapman, Chapman Industries
Far as I can tell, Autumn and Clay got along just fine
last night. They went off into a corner for part of the
time but looked like they were just talking.
I must say, though, that little gal of yours has sure
grown up.

All the best,
Fred

FAX
To: Debra Reese
From: Jackie Dutton
Dear Ms. Reese,
Thanks ever so for giving me the contact number for
Garth Rivers. Autumn didn't act like she minded. In
fact, she probably didn't even notice. She and Clay
are DEFINITELY back together.

Love,
Jackie Dutton

FAX
To: Debra, Reese Ranch
From: Margaret Schwertner, Rocking S Ranch

Dear Debra,

I'll expect an engagement announcement momentarily! Yes! You should have been there. Autumn has stars in her eyes where Clay is concerned and he obviously adores her. I swear, it brought tears to my eyes. They are perfect for each other.

All my love,
Maggie

FAX
To: Debra Reese, Reese Ranch
From: Nellie Barnett, Golden B
Debra, the reports so far are all fabulous! How are things at your end?

N.

FACSIMILE
To: Nellie
From: Debra
They're still asleep at my end!

Anxiously,
Debra

THE incessant beeping of the fax machine finally dragged Autumn from her bed. The ringing she'd ignored, but now the stupid thing was out of paper.

She squinted at the clock. It wasn't terribly early, but her mother was probably still outside doing chores. Sighing, Autumn stuffed her arms into her robe and shuffled down the hall to the spare bedroom that served as the ranch office.

She'd actually been awake for a while, thinking about Clay. He'd left right after he'd told her he loved her, not even waiting to see if she'd tell him she loved him back.

He wanted her to think about it first.

She opened the supply closet and got a new roll of fax paper. Clay was proving far more clever than she'd ever given him credit for, because her first instinct had been to blurt out that she loved him, too. In fact, it was also her second and third instinct.

But Clay obviously wanted a declaration in the clear light of day. She smiled to herself. He just might get his wish.

"Good grief, look at all this." So many faxes had come in that they'd spilled over onto the floor.

Autumn opened the cover of the fax machine and inserted the paper so the incoming fax could be printed, then gathered up the curling sheets of paper.

They were all reports on her evening with Clay! "Oh, Mom!" Autumn laughed.

Debra had been so calm last night, only casually asking if Autumn had had a good time, when in reality, she must have been dying for information.

"Serves you right for sending out your spies."

Autumn sat on the edge of the desk and started reading, chuckling at the descriptions. Fortunately, no one had reported seeing her kissing Clay behind the coatroom, which was what she'd been afraid she'd find.

There were three requests asking where Autumn had bought her dress. "I'll never tell," she murmured to herself.

It also appeared that her mother and Mrs. Barnett had been keeping in close contact, as well.

Autumn picked up the wad of faxes in the file box, working her way backward until she got to one that referred to the Yellow Rose. *I'm calling the Yellow Rose to find out how much it will cost to get them to admit they made a mistake in not matching those two.* It was dated before the second visit she and Clay had paid to the Yellow Rose.

Wait a minute. Autumn read the fax twice. Then a third time as anger made her hands shake. Clay's mother had bribed the Yellow Rose to match them together?

Their magical evening had been fake?

Autumn felt like the most gullible human being in the world. Their parents had been trying to get them together one way or another for years, and it was obvious that they still were.

How could Clay stand it—or was he in on it?

How dare they? Angry tears formed in her eyes, but she wiped them away and read the fax beneath that one, expecting to see more of the Yellow Rose plot.

The word "selling" stopped her cold. *This ranch was always Ben's dream—or rather his father's. Now that they're both gone, I realized I was keeping things going for Autumn—and she's not interested, not really. And you must know that hiring a foreman made this a losing operation.*

Autumn had assumed that her father's insurance money was covering the cost of a foreman. *But you never asked, did you?* prodded an inner voice. Still, why hadn't her mother said anything?

Autumn quickly flipped through the faxes until she found the one offering first right of refusal to the Golden B.

Clay had never said anything. And he must have known. In fact, that was probably why he'd gone along with his parents' plans. Marry Autumn and then they wouldn't have to buy the ranch.

How could he stand being used that way?

How could he justify telling her he loved her?

Because everyone knew Autumn wouldn't agree to marry Clay unless she believed she was in love with him.

Feeling cold, she wrapped her robe tightly around her. She didn't know what she felt anymore.

Autumn searched for anything more about the sale and found another Yellow Rose fax. *I'm giving the Yellow Rose a call and demanding that they recalculate their forms, or whatever they do to match people.* So typical of Clay's mother.

That was it, then. She and Clay hadn't really been matched together. It was all a setup because they knew she wouldn't go out with him otherwise.

A tear dripped onto the flimsy fax paper. All she'd ever wanted was the freedom to make her own life choices instead of having them dictated to her by circumstances and expectations.

No matter how much she'd pleaded over the years, it was obvious that her mother still didn't trust her to make those important decisions if they differed from what she had in mind for her daughter. Debra was still manipulating, and now Clay and his family were plotting with her.

Clay. Another tear fell. Did he or did he not know of all this?

And…did he really love her?

She had to find out.

"Mo-ther!" Hopping off the desk, Autumn stormed through the house.

"I'm in the kitchen," Debra called.

"Do you mind explaining this?" Autumn demanded, and threw the faxes on the kitchen table. The bouquet of yellow roses sat in the center, its blooms now starting to droop.

Debra had just come in the back door and was taking off her work gloves. "I mind the tone of voice you're using with me."

"I'm sorry."

Nodding, Debra hung her coat on the peg by the door. "All right, what's wrong?"

"Everything!" Autumn wailed, and pointed to the faxes. "You—you're selling the ranch and you didn't even tell me?"

"I'm thinking of putting it on the market, yes. I would've told you before anything had been decided." Debra calmly poured herself a cup of coffee and one for Autumn, as well. "I've offered it to Hank and Nellie. If we agree on a price, then I won't have to list the property."

"But why?"

Debra looked straight at her. "Are you willing to stay here and run the ranch with me?"

Choices. You wanted choices. Here's one. Did she intend to run the ranch with her mother? Not merely contribute income, but handle the never-ending daily chores and responsibilities? Did she intend to give up her law career before it ever got started?

"No." Autumn couldn't speak in more than a whisper, conscious that a chapter was closing in her life.

"That's why I'm selling." Debra looked at her a moment, then continued, her voice softer. "You've been back here over a year and it's taken all your salary and then some to keep the place going. What's the point if it isn't what you want to do?"

"But you shouldn't have to lose your home."

Debra walked over to the table, set her coffee cup down and sifted through the faxes, removing one. "I said it all here—this place was a dream of Ben's father. Ben loved it, and I did, too, when he was alive. But ranching is all I've ever known. I'd like to see what else is out there in the world." She smiled. "Just like my daughter."

"Oh, Mom." Autumn found herself in her mother's comforting arms. "If you change your mind and want to stay here, please tell me. I can take a full-time job if it will help."

"I'm not going to change my mind," Debra said. "And I don't want you to, either."

FAX
To: Debra Reese, Owner
 Reese Ranch
From: Henry Barnett and Eleanor Winters Barnett, Owners
 Golden B Ranch, Incorporated
Number of pages: 3
Please consider the attached terms our

formal bid for the property known as Reese Ranch (legal description attached). As per the original sales agreement, you have thirty days to accept or decline this offer.

Very truly yours,
Henry Barnett
Eleanor Winters Barnett

FAX
To: Henry Barnett and Eleanor Winters Barnett, Owners
    Golden B Ranch, Incorporated
From: Debra Reese, Owner
    Reese Ranch
Dear Nellie and Hank,
I don't need thirty days. I've spoken with Autumn and you've been more than generous. I accept.

Sincerely,
Debra

If Autumn had been honest with her mother, she would have told her what was really bothering her— the bribe to Yellow Rose Matchmakers.

But that was something she had to discuss with Clay first.

This was a day when she'd like to saddle a horse and ride for hours, but Clay's ranch house was too far away. So without giving him advance warning, Autumn drove over to the Barnetts'. She wanted to see Clay's face when she told him about their fraudulent pairing.

Nellie Barnett herself opened the door, her face wreathed in smiles. "Autumn, what a lovely surprise! Clay just came in for lunch. You'll join us, won't you?"

Autumn hadn't paid any attention to the time and now was embarrassed at arriving right at mealtime.

Before she could answer, Clay appeared, drying his hands on a kitchen towel. "'Lo, Autumn."

His voice was the same as always. The way he looked at her was not. In fact, the way he looked, period, was not the same. She'd never noticed the firm set of his jaw, nor the well-shaped mouth. And she knew his eyes hadn't gazed at her with such a banked intensity before.

Okay, so he was good-looking and a great kisser. That didn't change the fact that she'd been manipulated.

Maybe they both had.

Maybe Clay didn't know.

"I have an idea," Mrs. Barnett said while the two of them continued to stare at one another. "It's a nice sunny day. Why don't I fix you some sandwiches and you can eat on the patio?"

"Thanks, Mom."

Clay's mother took the towel from him as she returned to the kitchen.

As soon as the sound of his mother's footsteps faded, Clay closed the distance between them. "You've been thinking."

"Yes." Autumn knew her voice sounded strained.

"You want to sit down while you spit it out?"

It probably was pretty obvious that she was upset. Autumn nodded, then followed him into the den with the magnificent two-story stone fireplace. How many times had she been in this room over the years?

That didn't matter now.

"We were set up," she began, pulling the folded faxes out of her purse. "I found these this morning." She handed the papers concerning the Yellow Rose to Clay.

He read them, then handed them back.

"Well?" she demanded when he didn't say anything. "Did you know about this?"

"No."

"And it doesn't make you mad?"

"What's the big deal?"

"The big deal is that our mothers bribed the Yellow Rose to match us together."

"So what if they did?"

"So what? Then our match was a lie."

Clay leaned against the back of the leather couch and crossed his arms. "So? Were you going to let a computer pick your husband for you?"

He was missing the point. "I went to the Yellow Rose in good faith. I expected computer matches. They cheated."

"Do you know that for a fact?"

She shook the papers at him. "How much more fact do you need?"

"I mean, have you called the Yellow Rose?"

"No, but I intend to."

He smiled and shook his head. "Go ahead, but it doesn't matter to me if that's what it took for you to realize that we belong together." He tried to take her in his arms, but she wiggled free.

Belong together. It was the "sacred trust" theory

all over again. "Did you know that my mother offered to sell our ranch to your parents?"

He blinked. "Yes."

A queasy feeling settled in Autumn's stomach. "How long?"

"A while."

"And you never bothered to tell me?"

"It wasn't my place to. That was between you and your mother."

"Okay." She stuffed the faxes back into her purse. "I'll concede that. But it's still just one more way people have been manipulating me, and I'm sick of it."

He narrowed his eyes. "You know, Autumn, everything in this world isn't just about you and what you want and what you feel. Other people have their own feelings and their own lives."

"Then I wish they'd live them and leave me alone!"

"I believe that's exactly what your mother is trying to do."

"You didn't see all the faxes that came in this morning. Practically everyone who was at the ball last night was spying for her."

Clay had gone stone-faced.

It took a few seconds before Autumn figured out that he was angry. She'd never seen Clay blazingly angry before. It wasn't something she wanted to see often.

"I understand what this is all about. You're looking for excuses to avoid making a decision about us." Autumn started to say something, but he cut her off. "Yes, us! Last night I told you I loved you and

I'm pretty certain you love me, too, but you're too hardheaded to admit it. You talk a good line about wanting choices, but you don't really. You want to be forced into a decision so you don't have to accept responsibility for it.''

"That's not true!"

"Okay, then try this. Marry me. Yes, or no. That's your choice, but I'm not waiting around forever for you to make it.''

And he walked off, his boot heels loud against the stone-tile floor.

Autumn stared after him, stunned. How could he say those things to her?

She didn't stay for lunch but got back in her Bronco and drove home. She didn't turn into the driveway but continued on into San Antonio and straight to the Yellow Rose. Once there, she ran up the steps and pushed open the door. A new bouquet of yellow roses filled the ginger-jar vase in the foyer.

"Hey, what are you doing back here?" Maria called from the parlor where she was showing another young woman the scrapbook. "Did you bring us an invitation to the wedding?"

"No." Unsmiling, Autumn once again withdrew the faxes. "I'd like you to explain something to me."

"I'll just let you look through our letters from satisfied clients," Maria told the young woman and rose to her feet.

Once again, Autumn found herself in the back office.

"You don't look so good," Maria said.

"I don't feel so good," Autumn answered. "I found these faxes that indicate the Yellow Rose was bribed to match me with Clayton Barnett." She held them out to Maria.

"Nope."

"Don't you even want to read them?"

"Don't have to. The lady called and I told her no." Maria shook her finger as though Autumn was a naughty little girl. "And I have to tell you, I don't like you coming in here with your stormy face and accusing me of taking a bribe!"

"I...I'm sorry," Autumn found herself apologizing.

"You should be. You were matched with that nice handsome man just the way the computer said. But you two don't need a computer. You were in love with each other when you first came here."

"No." Autumn shook her head. "No, we definitely weren't."

Maria shrugged. "Maybe yes, maybe no. But you are now, right?"

Autumn didn't answer.

Maria gave her a stern look. "You haven't gone and done something stupid on account of thinking you weren't really matched together, have you?"

In her mind's eye, Autumn saw Clay's angry face as he'd proposed to her.

Proposed to her!

The man she loved and who loved her had proposed to her.

And what had she answered?

She stared from the faxes to Maria. "Yes, I've gone and done something very stupid. Incredibly stupid. We're talking stupidity of titanic proportions."

"I figured as much. So what are you going to do about it?"

"Maria, I've been so incredibly stupid, I don't think there's anything I can do. No matter what anyone thinks, or what anyone does—even if you had fixed the computer results—"

"Hey!"

"I know you didn't, but even if we went out together because you had, if we love each other, it shouldn't matter, right?"

Maria held her head. "You're making me dizzy, but I think so."

"What do I do now?" Autumn groaned.

"Well, you've got to go to him then and try to convince him you're not as stupid as you think you are."

"I can't do that."

"Why not? Did he tell you he never wanted to see you again?"

"No. He proposed."

"Marriage?" Maria stared at her. "And what did you say?"

Autumn twisted the papers she held. "I didn't say anything."

Muttering in Spanish, Maria threw up her arms. "You go back and you say yes!"

"It's not that simple."

Maria started pushing her down the hall. "So you say yes and then you kiss him. Trust me. It's that simple."

Could it be? Even after she'd acted like the biggest, most self-centered fool in the universe?

"Wait." Maria plucked a yellow rose from the vase in the foyer. "Take this for luck."

Autumn took the rose. She was afraid she'd need all the luck she could get. After stopping for gas, she drove straight to Clay's ranch house before she lost her nerve.

"Hello, Autumn." Once more, Clay's mother greeted her, but this time, her smile was no more than polite.

Clutching the yellow rose, Autumn stammered, "Is—is Clay here?"

"He's in the calving barn."

The walk to the calving barn was the longest Autumn ever remembered taking. She felt Nellie Barnett watching her the entire way.

Autumn knew Clay well enough to know that he hadn't told his mother what words they'd exchanged, but Mrs. Barnett had sensed that her son was upset and knew Autumn was the cause of it.

She found him bottle-feeding an orphaned calf. "'Lo, Clay," she said, and leaned on the wooden railing.

"Autumn." He tilted his head back until he could see out from under his hat brim.

Maria had said this would be simple. This wasn't simple at all.

He nodded toward the yellow rose she twirled in her hands. "Been into San Antonio?"

"Yes."

"And?"

"And I've been really stupid."

"They didn't mess with the computer, did they?"

She shook her head.

"Mom said they wouldn't. I lit into her pretty good for even trying, though."

Autumn felt like dirt. "Well, that isn't all I've been stupid about. You were right—"

"Say that part again."

"You were right," she repeated heavily through gritted teeth. "It shouldn't have mattered. I *was* looking for a reason not to admit that everybody had been right all along. I mean, how could they figure it out before I could?"

"You weren't ready to." The calf had finished the bottle and Clay stood, brushing the hay from his jeans. "No shame in that." He came out of the stall and latched it.

"But there's plenty of shame in throwing a hissy fit over nothing. And I'm sorry."

He smiled down at her. "Is that all?"

"Oh." She handed him the rose. "Yes."

"Yes?"

She nodded. "My choice. I choose yes—you."

He stared hard at her. "You're not saying you'll marry me because you're afraid of losing your home, are you?"

"No!"

"Because I can't afford to buy it."

Autumn stared back at Clay—at her future. "I love you, not the ranch. I don't care if I have a ranch. I don't care if *you* have a ranch. I care if we're together."

Clay gathered her to him in a fierce hug. "That's the first time you've told me you love me. Autumn, I swear, you are the most challenging woman, but you *are* worth the wait. I hope you just meant what you said.''

''I did.''

''Good, because although *I* couldn't afford to buy your ranch, my dad could. And did.''

The sale had gone through? ''Why didn't you tell me?''

''Because knowing you, you would have thought it was like buying you, right? And doggone it, it was just too good of a piece of property to let pass into other hands.''

''Wait a minute—you mean that you let him buy it even though you knew I might accuse you of trying to keep me around?''

''You're looking at it backwards. We own it—or will soon. Your mother has already told us she wants to move into town. You're actually going to be farther away.''

He was right. ''Then I guess we'd better hurry up the wedding or I'll find myself out on the side of the road.''

Clay laughed. ''Sounds good to me. But what about your school?''

''I can commute or take correspondence courses, or both.''

''You've got everything all worked out. I have to tell you that I'm relieved to hear that.''

''I had plenty of time to think on the drive back from the Yellow Rose.''

He laughed.

''Oh, Clay?''

''Mmm?''

''Maria said I should kiss you.''

"Maria is a wise woman," he declared, and low-ered his lips to hers.

YELLOW ROSE MATCHMAKERS
MATCH EVALUATION

NAME OF DATE: *Clayton Barnett*

ACTIVITY: *Champion Buyers' Ball*

WOULD YOU DATE THIS PERSON AGAIN? *Yes.*

WHY OR WHY NOT? *I want to date him for the rest of my life.*

DID YOU FIND ATTRIBUTES OF THIS MATCH THAT ARE INCOMPATIBLE WITH TRAITS YOU DESIRE IN A MATE? BE SPECIFIC. A PERSONALITY PROFILE IS ENCLOSED FOR YOUR REFERENCE. *He's perfect.*

YELLOW ROSE MATCHMAKERS
MATCH EVALUATION

NAME OF DATE: *Autumn Reese*

ACTIVITY: *Buyers' Ball*

WOULD YOU DATE THIS PERSON AGAIN? *You betcha.*

WHY OR WHY NOT? *I want to show her off.*

DID YOU FIND ATTRIBUTES OF THIS MATCH THAT ARE INCOMPATIBLE WITH TRAITS YOU DESIRE IN A MATE? BE SPECIFIC. A PERSONALITY PROFILE IS ENCLOSED FOR YOUR REFERENCE. *She can be a little hardheaded at times, but that's just go-ing to make life interesting.*

YELLOW ROSE MATCHMAKERS CLIENT FILE

NAME: Autumn Reese
STATUS: Moved to inactive, match successful.

YELLOW ROSE MATCHMAKERS CLIENT FILE

NAME: Clayton Barnett
STATUS: Moved to inactive, match successful.

FAX
To: Debra Reese, Reese Ranch
From: Nellie Barnett, Golden B
Dear Debra, These past few days have been so hectic, I don't know how you've been able to cope. I can't believe that after dawdling for years and years, our children want to get married in a matter of weeks. Can't you persuade them to wait until April or May?

Hopefully,
Nellie

FACSIMILE
To: Nellie Barnett, Golden B Ranch
From: Debra Reese, Reese Ranch
Think, Nellie dear. After what we've gone through, especially in the past few weeks, do you really want to risk delaying their wedding? I didn't think so.

Happily swamped with wedding plans,
Debra

FAX
To: Autumn Reese, Reese Ranch

Clay Loves Autumn
x x x

FACSIMILE
To: Clay Barnett, Golden B Ranch
From: Autumn Reese, Reese Ranch
Prove it. Nine o'clock at the old pecan tree. Bring your lips.

Question: How do you find the sexy cowboy of your dreams?

Answer: Read on....

Texas Grooms Wanted!
is a brand-new miniseries from

Harlequin Romance®

Meet three very special heroines who are all looking for very special Texas men—their future husbands! Good men may be hard to find, but these women have experts on hand. They've all signed up with the Yellow Rose Matchmakers. The oldest and the best matchmaking service in San Antonio, Texas, the Yellow Rose guarantees to find any woman her perfect partner....

So for the cutest cowboys in the whole state of Texas, look out for:

HAND-PICKED HUSBAND
by Heather MacAllister in January 1999

BACHELOR AVAILABLE!
by Ruth Jean Dale in February 1999

THE NINE-DOLLAR DADDY
by Day Leclaire in March 1999

Only cowboys need apply...

Available wherever
Harlequin Romance books
are sold.

MEN *at* WORK

All work and no play?
Not these men!

January 1999
SOMETHING WORTH KEEPING by Kathleen Eagle
He worked with iron and steel, and was as wild as the mustangs that were his passion. She was a high-class horse trainer from the East. Was her gentle touch enough to tame his unruly heart?

February 1999
HANDSOME DEVIL by Joan Hohl
His roguish good looks and intelligence drew women like magnets, but Luke Branson was having too much fun to marry again. Then Selena McInnes strolled before him and turned his life upside down!

March 1999
STARK LIGHTNING by Elaine Barbieri
The boss's daughter was ornery, stubborn and off-limits for cowboy Branch Walker! But Valentine was also nearly impossible to resist. Could they negotiate a truce...or a surrender?

Available at your favorite retail outlet!

MEN AT WORK™

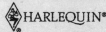 HARLEQUIN®  *Silhouette*®

Look us up on-line at: http://www.romance.net   PMAW4

Harlequin Romance®

We're proud to announce the "birth" of a brand-new series full of babies, bachelors and happy-ever-afters: *Daddy Boom*. Meet gorgeous heroes who are about to discover that there's a first time for everything—even fatherhood!

Starting in February 1999 we'll be bringing you one *Daddy Boom* title every other month.

February 1999: **BRANNIGAN'S BABY**
by Grace Green

April 1999: **DADDY AND DAUGHTERS**
by Barbara McMahon

We'll also be bringing you deliciously cute *Daddy Boom* books by Lucy Gordon, Kate Denton, Leigh Michaels and a special Christmas story from Emma Richmond.

Who says bachelors and babies don't mix?

Available wherever Harlequin books are sold.

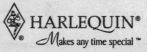

HARLEQUIN®
Makes any time special ™

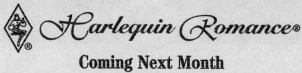

ℋarlequin Romance®

Coming Next Month

#3539 BACHELOR AVAILABLE! Ruth Jean Dale
Cody James was tall, sexy and handsome—he took Emily Kirkwood's
breath away. Too bad that Emily hadn't joined the Yellow Rose
Matchmakers to find a man but to write a Valentine's story on...
well...how to get a man. Only, Cody *was* available...and perhaps what
this story needed was a little in-depth research!

Texas Grooms Wanted! *Only cowboys need apply!*

#3540 BOARDROOM PROPOSAL Margaret Way
It's the job of her dreams, but can Eve Copeland believe that she won it
fairly and squarely? Her new boss, after all, has a secret he'd go to great
lengths to conceal....

#3541 HER HUSBAND-TO-BE Leigh Michaels
Deke Oliver was convinced Danielle was trying to manipulate him into
marriage—just because they'd jointly inherited a property...and were
forced to live together under the same roof! But Deke wasn't husband
material, and Danielle simply *had* to convince him that she wasn't
dreaming of wedding bells!

#3542 BRANNIGAN'S BABY Grace Green
When Luke Brannigan asked Whitney for help, she was torn. On the one
hand, she wanted to get as far away as possible from this annoyingly
gorgeous man, who insisted on flirting with her. On the other, how could
she refuse to help when Luke was obviously struggling to bring up his
adorable baby son?

Daddy Boom—*Who says bachelors and babies don't mix?*